Singing to Cuba

Margarita Engle

Arte Público Press
Houston
Texas
1993

M000083284

This book is made possible through a grant from the National Endowment for the Arts (a federal agency), the Lila Wallace -Reader's Digest Fund and the Andrew W. Mellon Foundation.

Arte Público Press
University of Houston
Houston, Texas 77204-2090

Cover design by Mark Piñón

Library of Congress Cataloging-in-Publication Data

Engle, Margarita M.
      Singing to Cuba / by Margarita M. Engle.
      p.   cm.
      ISBN 1-55885-070-8
      1. Cuban Americans–Travel–Cuba–Fiction.
I. Title.
PS3555.N4254S57 1993
813' .54–dc20   93-13446
                                                CIP

For Curtis, Victor and Nicole,

and

for the children of the Captive Towns

I am grateful to my husband and children for their patience, to my parents for sending me on childhood adventures to Cuba, and to my grandmother and other exiled relatives for reminiscing in my presence.

For encouragement I thank Charles Ericksen of Hispanic Link News Service, the late Dr. Tomás Rivera, Jerry and Carla Finch, Judy Carey, J.G., D.G., R.B., P.B., M. H. and P.H.

Thanks to everyone at Arte Público Press, and especially to Silvia Novo Pena for her editing and suggestions.

I am grateful to individuals and organizations investigating human rights violations in Cuba, and to historian Enrique Encinosa for documentation of events leading up to construction of the communities known as "*El Pueblo Cautivo*," the "Captive Towns."

For inspiration I thank the "Singers to Cuba."

For angels and hope I thank God.

De músico, poeta y loco
Todos tenemos un poco

Of musician, poet and lunatic
We each contain a streak

Cuban folk saying

All is beautiful and constant,
all is music and reason,
and all, like the diamond,
before it is light is coal.

José Martí

AUTHOR'S NOTE

Singing to Cuba is a work of fiction. With the exception of well-known historical figures, all characters are imaginary; any resemblance to real persons, living or dead, is entirely coincidental.

I wrote this novel because outside of Cuba very few people know about the Captive Towns, and inside Cuba very few dare speak of them.

Margarita M. Engle
California, 1993

Singing to Cuba

During the summer of 1991, I slipped into Cuba to tell my relatives they are not forgotten. It was not a pronouncement I could have conceived alone, but a message entrusted to me by an angel who came to me while I was singing, and enveloped me like a shadow, with wings as soft as the embrace of smoke after fire in a dream, with a voice more touch than sound.

I am not a mystic, but merely a farm wife who occasionally writes brief, insignificant poems about the small creatures of nature, birds, frogs, snails, moths. I grew up in Spanish Harlem, a smoker of opium and dreamer of dragons and mermaids, but now, returning to the healing influence of the land and of crops, I live with my husband and children on a peaceful farm in a place still referred to, with nostalgia, as the Wild West.

On quiet mornings I write letters on behalf of political prisoners trapped in the dungeons of distant lands, mysterious places still ruled by evil kings who resemble those enumerated in the Old Testament.

When I am at home in my rural corner of the big North, I dedicate my hours to observing the movements of clouds and leaves, the decay of blossoms, the ripening of fruit. My task is profoundly satisfying, although futile. When I am immersed in the dry sunlight and soil, I feel that I have been transformed into the echo of a sweet melancholy song reverberating across the sea, the rustle of green sugarcane, the twirl of dancing palms, hot copper sun, soil the color of blood.

Every month I receive batches of human rights bulletins, with instructions for letters. I copy the letters and address them to Your Excellency or Your Highness. Many of these bulletins describe in detail the tortures imposed on the flesh of humans arrested for the intonation of a voice, a phrase or a verse, or for being the distant cousin of an opponent of the regime. The letters demand freedom and justice.

Some of the prisoners are held in dungeons beneath the fortress of La Cabaña in Havana, on the alligator-shaped isle I think of as enchanted, where, long ago, amid the rustle of green sugarcane and the twirl of dancing palms, much of my memory was trapped.

Tourists from Europe and Canada stroll along the stones of the

fortress, photographing one another posed alongside the dark cylinders of
cannon left behind by Imperial Spain, gun barrels still pointed away from
the island, powerless to defend it against the warfare within, a silent battle
of the spirit.

The dungeons are filled with ordinary Cubans arrested by State Security on charges of "disrespect" or "dangerousness" or for attempting to flee
the island on a raft, or for possession of "enemy propaganda," a cartoon
perhaps, or a poem, a careless joke.

The cases are numerous and astonishing. For instance, one man was
arrested by State Security in1982. He was sentenced to eight years in
prison under Article 108 of the Cuban Penal Code, on charges of receiving
enemy propaganda in the form of a letter from his cousin in the North, a
letter containing newspaper clippings judged to be criticizing the government of Fidel Castro Ruz, *Presidente de la República* and *Líder Máximo*, self-
proclaimed Maximum Leader.

So, as you in the North might imagine, I try to exercise extreme caution
when I write to my cousin Miguelito in Havana, or to my great-aunt Isabelita in Trinidad, or to my great-uncle Daniel in his remote village on the head
of the alligator. As far as my distant cousins in the Captive Towns are con-
cerned, it is better for them if they never receive any letters from the North.

Not long after I returned from slipping into Cuba to tell my relatives
they are not forgotten, I received a bulletin documenting the arrest and
torture of Omar, one of my grandmother's cousins, brother of Alvaro,
Emilio and Adán, who rebelled, hiding in the mountains, before a veil of
deep melancholy fell across the enchanted isle. I was sitting in the North,
opening my mail and enjoying the arid sunlight, when suddenly I recognized the name of my grandmother's cousin, arrested on charges of *peligrosidad*, dangerousness, as defined by Section XI of the Cuban Penal Code, the
"special proclivity of a person to commit crimes."

Of course, Omar had not actually committed a "crime against the
State," but he had been perceived as a person capable of doing so if given
the chance. For this reason, his freedom was denied him in advance, to
avoid temptation. He had, after all, been spotted by State Security agents
at a meeting of human rights activists in some remote corner on the head
of the alligator.

Omar was detained for several months in the punishment cell of a
hospital psychiatric ward.

Electroshock treatments were administered on a wet floor with criminally insane inmates acting as orderlies. Omar was not diagnosed insane by any doctor, but was classified as potentially "indifferent to Socialism" and was said to be suffering from delusions regarding his ability to alter the circumstances of his life.

The case of my distant cousin Omar is only one of many. For instance, there is the case of a man who belonged to a human rights committee and was arrested in1989 because he was believed to be planning a demonstration. Once they had him in prison for suspicion of planning a criminal activity, they also convicted him of illicit economic activity on the grounds that he had been hiring himself out as a photographer, a violation of restrictions against private enterprise.

And the case of María Elena Cruz Varela, poet and president of an opposition group which calls itself "Alternative View." She was the author of the group's "Declaration of Cuban Intellectuals," an open letter circulated during May, 1991, calling for freedom to conduct a broad national debate, direct elections and the release of political prisoners. As a result, the poet was subjected to repeated "Acts of Repudiation" during which mobs organized by State Security agents dragged her down several flights of stairs, beat her and forcibly stuffed her writings into her mouth, making her swallow them. On November 27 she was tried, convicted and sentenced to two years in prison for defaming state institutions and holding illegal meetings.

Before her arrest the poet wrote, "We are almost at the beginning of the end," and another member of her group added, "Please put an SOS out for Cuba. You who are sensible men, do not permit this island to sink into the ocean, or this mad Pied Piper to lead us all to the water's edge."

Of course, it is very difficult to obtain accurate details of every arrest, because witnesses are afraid to speak. In fact, sometimes witnesses are also afraid not to speak. In1990 a man was arrested and charged with not informing on a friend who tried to leave the country without permission.

So, you can see that life in Cuba is very dangerous and, as you can imagine, if you allow yourself to imagine such horrors, the entire island has been silenced by fear.

The first time I went to Cuba I was small, a mere toddler. During that summer of 1953, Fidel Castro Ruz, Maximum Leader, made his first attack against the army of the previous despot, Fulgencio Batista, who had seized power himself, through a military coup, and who, like every Cuban dictator before and since, was believed to be something of a *Santero*, suspected of achieving power not only through armed invasions, but through black magic and the casting of spells.

My second visit to the accursed island was during the summer of 1960, when I was only eight years old, and the revolution itself was still new and inflated with triumphant illusions, lighter than air, like a balloon filled with helium, sailing away beyond reach.

And now, since my third trip to Cuba, in 1991, when an angel wrapped me in the shadow of tranquil wings, flashes of memory come to me across the sea, like fireflies, like meteors, like flying fish soaring above phosphorescent waves.

On the morning of his arrest, Gabriel stepped out into the quiet before dawn, smiled broadly, and shook his fist at the devil, as always.

He journeyed from the small tropical farm house to the corral, traversing a morass of fertile red mud infested with hookworms.

His two moustached sons were at his sides, as always. Together the three of them began the milking, and soon, as the sky reddened, the devil himself appeared on the green horizon, fuming.

I slipped into Cuba during a time referred to by the Maximum Leader as the prelude to "Option Zero." He called this prelude a "special period in time of peace." All over Havana, billboards advertised the special period as a time of ultimate sacrifice and perennial struggle. The signs used words like salvation and glory.

I remembered a time, during the summer of 1960, when my entire Cuban peasant family still thought of the revolution as a kind of miracle, promising paradise on earth, bringing an era of justice and freedom to an island that felt betrayed by perpetual bondage.

I was eight years old then, and with my cousins I played on the streets of Havana, watching the migrations of reptile-green truckloads of soldiers known as *Barbudos*, the bearded ones. All around us, the adults of our family were jubilant, cheering the soldiers who had triumphed against the horror of tyranny.

During the Special Period of 1991, the people listened to his speeches with a melancholy silence, applauding on cue. They glanced around to see which of the silent men in embroidered *guayabera* shirts might be political police, secret police, State Security. The shirts were white like clouds, pale blue like the crystalline ridges of waves on the sea, yellow like melons, like mangos, like the shells of moon snails, embroidered with tiny, delicate brown stitches.

Watching the melancholy people, the silent men, the Maximum Leader with his dramatic gestures and infuriated voice, memories pursued me like untamed horses on a galloping sky.

It was impossible to tell which of the silent men might be secret police. The people glanced around, hoping to avoid any disruptions of the ritual. If anyone spoke out, an Act of Repudiation would swiftly be organized by the silent men with their walkie-talkies and hidden weapons. The disruptive individual would be beaten, as an example.

The people glanced from chin to chin, avoiding eyes.

I scanned the crowd, remembering the early speeches, how long and glorious they had been, inspiring, replete with promises–toys for the children, freedom and justice for the adults, land for the peasants, food for all.

There had been poetry in those speeches, spirit and hope.

"When Fidel's troops marched into Havana," my great-uncle Gabriel had told me during the summer of 1960, while we watched the sunset on his sweet green farm, "white doves floated down from the clouds and landed on the hands of the Maximum Leader."

We were watching the red sunset when Gabriel gave me this vision of salvation. "The whole world," my great-uncle said, "seemed enveloped by wings, illuminated. We were in paradise."

Now, thirty-one years after my last visit, once again I was on my magical island, looking around, glancing from eyebrow to eyebrow, trying to discern which of the silent men might be secret police, which of the colorful embroidered shirts might conceal a weapon and a radio.

"Socialism or death!" an old woman shouted. Then she glanced around to make sure she had been heard and, having done her duty, she moved silently away, shoulders drooping, eyes drowned by waves of melancholy.

I left the crowd and walked through the familiar streets of Old Havana, past a billboard bearing the image of a bearded hero and the words, "To be like him!" Looking up, I found the ancient colonial buildings crumbling, their gargoyles, like lepers, suffering the loss of nose or chin. Thousands of carved marble angels graced the buildings and tombs of the city, immense white angels, with stone wings and silent, open singing mouths.

On the morning of his arrest, Gabriel grinned at the half-wild cat as she licked a drop of warm frothing milk from the red soil beneath a cow's udder.

Gabriel scanned the sweep of green hills, the dancing trees and galloping clouds. He inhaled the air with jubilation, hot, moist, wild air, the air of a farm given by God, scented with manure and sugar, air so deeply lapis-blue at noon and so violently red at sunset, so full of moonlight and meteors at night, that Gabriel loved the air the way he loved his own freedom, without ever imagining that either might suddenly vanish.

Gabriel's air was replete with the fragrance of wet pasture and wild guava. It made Gabriel feel more poet than farmer. It made him feel like singing in a voice so strong it could reach across the sea, across the sky.

I returned to the captive island at a time when people seemed to be living under a mysterious spell of silence. Communism had collapsed in Eastern Europe and was on the verge of collapse in the Soviet Union. The Cuban government was surviving without the benefits it had enjoyed just a few years earlier, when other communist nations were willing to take sugar as payment for petroleum and manufactured goods.

The fuel shortage had left Cuba's few automobiles silent. The crowded red and mustard-yellow buses known as *guaguas* were becoming more scarce each day, leaving crowds of silent people waiting on the streets, unable to complain for fear of arrest. Hundreds of thousands of bicycles were being imported from China to take the place of motorized vehicles. The entire island was moving about on foot or on bicycles, enveloped by an all-consuming silence.

So many tractors were idle that farmers were training oxen to replace them. The ration lines were running out of bread. The factories had no more raw materials.

How penetrating that silence became, like a huge devouring mouth or the last poof of colored smoke at the end of a magician's final act.

Soon the Cuban people would be expected to proceed from their Special Period, the time of waiting, to a period the Maximum Leader referred to as Option Zero, a time of not existing, a time of total sacrifice, survival without food or fuel.

All over Havana, the long, sinuous ration lines struck me as a deliberate scheme to keep the people busy, to keep them obsessed by hunger, keep them quiet, fearful, expectant.

Slipping into Cuba at a time like this would have been extremely difficult, if the Maximum Leader had not decided to seek foreign currency by promoting tourism. I signed up for a tour of the island, then evaded my official guides, and went off on my own, exploring the alligator-shaped island, digging up the buried treasure of voices.

All over the island, I encountered angels and demons battling. Beneath them, the people struggled to find food for the day, transportation to and from their government jobs, clothes, shoes, hope.

I was reminded of a shrub my great-uncle Gabriel once showed me, a wild shrub which grows in the dark forested mountains of Cuba, where remnants of great groves of rare trees still survive—mahogany, ebony, cedar. The shrub is said to be so poisonous that even its shade will make a person sleep. The entire island, so quiet, shadowed by so many wings and talons, seemed to be asleep, as if more than ten million inhabitants had wandered together into that shady forest refuge and tasted the venom .

The things which happen in Cuba seem impossible. When I am at home in the North, under a Wild West sky, reading the human rights bulletins which arrive like clockwork every month, I am astonished by the variety of faces despair has found on the island. I am horrified, like the great nineteenth-century Cuban poet Jose Martí, who wrote about reaching out with horror and jubilation to touch an extinguished star which fell in front of his door. I read the bulletins and reach out, horrified and jubilant, to touch the meteorites of memory falling all around me.

In early 1984 two young men from San José de las Lajas were executed by firing squad for tossing nails onto the Havana-Santa Clara Highway.

Five lawyers were sentenced to death, and one, known to be a defender of political prisoners, died mysteriously in prison, reportedly of a heart attack, soon after his death sentence was commuted.

In 1980 the friend of a cartoonist was detained and charged with attempting to send his friend's drawings abroad. The artist was also arrested and sentenced to five years. The friend was sentenced to eight years, under Article 108.1 of the Cuban Penal Code, which classifies cartoons as enemy propaganda.

The silence in Havana in 1991 was absolute, a silence so complete that all conversations were whispered. In 1960 the streets had been filled with street musicians, vendors, huddles of gossiping women, groups of men smoking cigars and discussing politics. Already hundreds of alleged opponents, *anti-Castristas*, had been sent to the firing squads but the all-pervasive fear of later years had not yet seized the islanders' hearts.

I remembered the island as an enchanted place of green fields and lapis-blue sky, where *guajiro* peasants like my great-uncle Gabriel and his grown sons would challenge each other to demonstrations of roping skills one day, and duels of impromptu poetry the next.

In 1991 I found the island as beautiful as ever, the royal palms just as graceful, the *flamboyán* flowers as brilliantly crimson, the green of sugar cane as intense, the air as thick and wet and sweet, making me want to sing.

Yet the silence disturbed me in a way I could not explain. In 1960 Cuba had been a raucous island, men cursing, children shrieking, strangers singing on the streets, everyone talking loud and fast, everyone talking all at once, no one listening. The Cuban accent is rapid, a peculiar Andalusian accent brought by Columbus' sailors, embroidered with indigenous Taíno-Arawak words, and with expressions transported to the island from Nigeria and the Congo in the mouths of chained slaves. Cubans speak as if each carries a precious gold ball inside his mouth, a treasure never to be swallowed. They omit many of their consonants, creating a rhythmic musical language of vowels and staccato. Cubans speak with their hands and with their faces, with eyebrows and lips dancing.

In the countryside they still use archaic words brought from Spain by Columbus' men, measuring distance in leagues and land in *caballerías*, each *caballería* being thirty-three-and-a-third acres, the amount of land awarded to a knight errant for a deed of valor.

The sailors of Columbus' day were men who believed in mermaids. They believed in giant octopi capable of swallowing entire ships, and enormous wicked sea serpents. The sailors thought music could soothe the giant reptiles of the sea and, whenever they found themselves in a storm, with no musicians on board, they listened to the melodies of stars for comfort, swearing that those distant heavenly voices could be heard clearly despite the boundaries of time and distance.

———⌒∿⌒———

On the morning of his arrest Gabriel watched his two grown sons with pride and apprehension, chuckling at the antics of the lighthearted one showing off his rope tricks, and fearing for the fate of the serious one with his ancient indigenous nickname and daring voice. Never once did he imagine that both might be equally endangered. Both were good riders and cattlemen, self-sufficient guajiros endowed with Gabriel's own love of farming. Each would inherit a few caballerías of red soil for growing wild pasture, green sugarcane, and the groves of fruit trees that had always fed the guajiros even during the bad years when sugar prices plummeted.

Gabriel felt exhausted from his fear of sleep, his anxiety about the rumors circulating from one farm to another. It was said the Maximum Leader's troops were devouring entire regions, livestock, crops, even the guajiros themselves. Not a single bohío hut was being spared from the place called One Hundred Fires, Cienfuegos, to Trinity, Trinidad.

Gabriel looked at his own bohío with its palm-bark walls and palm-thatch roof, thinking things could not possibly be as bad as the rumors portrayed them, thinking it must be the exaggeration of passionate Cubans, always ready to dramatize the truth with fancy words and dancing hands.

Anyway, Gabriel felt safe. Hadn't he fed the troops when they were still ragged bands of bearded rebels hiding in the mountains? Hadn't he given them shelter when they passed through on their way to ambush the old tyrant's army outposts? Hadn't he shown them the best trails to take during the rainy season when only a real guajiro could find his way through the mountains? He'd expected no reward and asked for no payment. The rebels promised liberty, equality and fraternity, just as they were shown by the single star on the phrygian cap crowning Cuba's coat-of-arms, with its picture of the sun setting over the horizon of a blue sea, its key of gold to show how the island was like a key in the ocean, opening up the New World, its bands of blue and white representing honor, dignity and integrity, and the single silver-trunked royal palm with its graceful ballerina-skirt of fronds, symbolizing the strength and resilience of the Cuban people who bend like palm trees to keep from being broken by powerful hurricane winds.

There were some who said it was dangerous business feeding Fidel's rebels but Gabriel still hoped he'd had been right. The rebels had triumphed, the old tyrant had fled, and now it was just a matter of waiting to see whether the new bearded liberator would keep his promises or turn out to be another tyrant himself. If the rumors were true, Gabriel thought, then the future would be grim because each tyrant seemed to stay in power a little longer than the last one, and each rebellion seemed to consume more blood, more time, more passionate words. If the rumors were true, if people were really disappearing, if animals were really being slaughtered, houses destroyed, fields burned, what would become of the peasants, the people?

Gabriel wondered whether they could hide in the caves beneath their farm, make a last stand of defiance, fight off any new tyrant with machetes and hunting rifles. But no, Gabriel decided, the rumors could not be true. The bearded Comandante they'd fed and sheltered along with his rebels did not seem like a man so devious that he would turn against the very peasants who had supported him when he was weak, the people whose hopes had strengthened him in exchange for those promises of freedom. honor, dignity, integrity, liberty, equality, fraternity. Surely the man who'd used so many eloquent words, the man who was graced with white doves when he spoke, the man whose very name meant loyalty, that man Fidel would not reward his friends, the peasants, with such horrors.

———— ⌀ ————

I slipped onto the bewitched island pretending I only wanted to see the sights, the ancient walls of El Morro Castle and La Cabaña Fortress, the marble monuments, winged statues, beaches, caves, jungles, waterfalls, and the cane fields with their dirt roads that resembled veins.

In Cuba, in 1991, tourists could do anything they wanted, see anything they wanted, as long as they stayed away from the Cuban people. Soldiers were posted on the beaches to make sure the fishermen didn't try to have conversations with affluent foreigners. Secret police surrounded the hotels, patrolling the lobbies and shops to make sure Cubans didn't try to ask outsiders for information or assistance, to make sure the islanders never had a chance to tell their life stories, or to ask the tourists to smuggle letters to relatives in Miami, or poems, or paintings, or songs.

The tourists rode in air conditioned tour buses imported from Europe. They were free to hire Soviet-built Tourist-Taxis. Tourists carried specially made tourist coins designed with pretty ornaments, spiral snail shells, tropical blossoms, hummingbirds. The tourists were allowed to buy anything they wanted.

The Cuban people rode in crowded *guagua* buses, carried Cuban pesos bearing a portrait of the Maximum Leader addressing an immense crowd of loyal subjects, his arms extended in a dramatic gesture of benevolence. I had heard Fidel say, "¡*No soy caudillo!*" raising a finger to emphasize his claim, and I had to wonder whether he actually believed his own words, "I am not a dictator." *Caudillo* was a medieval word, a term evoking images of feudal landlords and tenant farmers, of royal decrees being read from parchment scrolls.

To me, the Maximum Leader now seemed even more antiquated than a *caudillo*. He seemed to have taken on the aspect of an Old Testament king, and I couldn't help thinking that the island's pervasive silence was a plague like the plagues of the Bible, like locusts, frogs or famine.

Walking alone through Havana's ominous silence, momentarily free of the official tour guides who kept trying to control my movements, I had no fear of an approaching rebellion. Instead, I expected to see bolts of lightning sent down from heaven to strike the evil monarch. I would not have been surprised to see Fidel transformed, like Nebuchadnezzar, into a beast, circling his walled city in the form of a wild animal.

The buildings of Havana were almost entirely free of graffitti, but the sight of a detached human finger writing prophecies on a stone wall would not have startled me. Surrounded by profound silence, such prophecies would have seemed more natural than terrorism or sabotage.

In my purse I carried the addresses of relatives I hadn't seen since my last visit in 1960. None of them had seen me since the months just before and just after my ninth birthday. They could not be expected to recognize or welcome me. I would not recognize them either. Perhaps they would think of me as a stranger, a *Yanqui* outsider with no business showing up after so many years of absence. Perhaps they would turn out to be happy on the island, desiring no contact with the world beyond. I had often heard North American idealists refer to Cuba as a worker's paradise, where medical care and education were free. I knew that most of my relatives were employed by the government, that all of the younger people had been educated by the State and that most were now professionals in education and medicine.

In New York, my uncle Juan and grandmother Amparo, who'd left the island shortly after Gabriel's arrest, seldom spoke about what had happened in Cuba. They told me Gabriel had been arrested and charged with counter-revolutionary activity but, beyond that, they seemed to know little about the incident, and everyone in my family accepted Gabriel's imprisonment as one of those things that couldn't be changed or understood. Nevertheless, every time I received a human rights bulletin, I wondered about Gabriel's arrest, whether he had received a fair trial, whether he was treated well in prison, and what had become of his family, the two strong moustached *guajiro* boys I remembered as daredevil cowboys always ready to challenge each other to a rodeo, yet eloquent enough to improvise songs and poems whenever there was a celebration on the farm. What had become of the others, Gabriel's wife and daughters, his grandchildren?

Although officially tourists were told they could travel freely throughout the island during the silent vigil of 1991, any who strayed from the hotel zones and guided tour groups were watched closely by quiet men in *guayaberas*, by hotel maids, waiters and taxi drivers.

As soon as I arrived in Cuba I became aware that I was being followed and watched. I had entered the country with as many suitcases as I could carry, each laden with innumerable small gifts for my relatives, fragrant soaps, colorful foil-wrapped candies and packages of chewing gum, raisins, combs, underwear, cans of condensed milk, pens and stationery, all small, inconspicuous items impossible to obtain on the island, but valued by those old enough to recall the pre-revolutionary years and treasured even more by the young, who had never seen such an abundance of small treasures.

I was nervous about my luggage, thinking the Customs Inspectors might immediately spot me as a Cuban-American visiting without the proper permits. They might suspect me of black marketeering.

In fact, it was illegal for me to enter private homes after coming to Cuba without admitting that I was Cuban-American, and without the proper permits, permits which were extremely difficult to obtain. For me, a relative of Gabriel's, they were forbidden.

Standing in line at the airport, anxiously awaiting my Customs Inspection, I thought of all the times I had called Cuban diplomats in the U.S., requesting permission to visit relatives on the island. Each time I had been answered with the emphatic words, "¡Absolutamente no!" . I had written to the Cuban Interests Section of the Czechoslovakian Embassy, to Marazul Tours, administered by the Cuban government from Miami and New York, to top news correspondents representing big international magazines. I had tried every avenue of application, negotiation and pleading, only to end up with the same answer every time, "¡Absolutamente no!" During many years of refusals, I had first lost the chance to see Gabriel, who died shortly after his release from prison, and then his brother Miguel, who died just a few months before I finally gave up on all the proper avenues of approach, and simply signed up for a recreational tour, along with several dozen adventurous European windsurfers, scuba divers and spelunkers. Cuba was, after all, still endowed with some of the world's most glorious tropical beaches and with vast networks of unexplored limestone caverns.

I went to the island with my relatives' addresses hidden in the depths of a big zippered bag I intended to use as camera case, purse, and delivery sack for all the small gifts from my heavy suitcases.

Cubans, I knew from the tales told by refugees, were now allowed only one new set of clothes per year and one pair of shoes. Other items, like pens and paper, could only be obtained if they were listed in the individual's ration booklet, and then only when a supply came in, and only by waiting in line for hours on end. With Soviet aid rapidly diminishing, the supply of manufactured goods had dwindled to practically nothing. I was certain the small gifts would be appreciated.

As my turn for the Customs Inspection finally arrived, I pushed my heavy suitcases toward a young uniformed Inspector. She looked at me, and said, "Oh, go on through." The Inspector smiled at me sympathetically and I wondered whether she suspected that I was actually a Cuban-American trying to see relatives. Perhaps she, like so many Cubans, had family in the U.S., family living in a land officially regarded as enemy territory. Perhaps she understood my desire to visit, with or without permission.

Once I was settled in a luxurious beach hotel, surrounded by French and German snorkelers and big-game fishermen, I began my first efforts to get in touch with Miguelito, a second cousin I hadn't seen since he was four years old.

He would now be thirty-six. I knew he was married and had a child. I knew he still lived in his late father's house near Old Havana. I didn't know whether he would remember me. I'd gone to Cuba without notifying my relatives in advance, because I feared they might have problems if the government realized they were planning to receive an unauthorized visitor. I figured it was best for them to be able to claim ignorance. I had walked along the beaches near the hotel, and had been told by Cuban families that they had been expressly forbidden all contact with foreigners. Soldiers carrying automatic weapons patrolled the beaches, ready to make sure no Cubans tried to leave the island on rafts or inner tubes, and also to insure that Cubans did not converse with visitors from other countries.

I had already walked around Havana, sensing the silence and fear, and I knew utmost caution would be required if I was to visit relatives without endangering them. For me, as a U.S. citizen, the risks seemed less ominous. However, I realized the Cuban government often chose not to differentiate between native Cubans and their American-born descendants. If they decided I was dangerous because of my relation to Gabriel, difficulties could result.

I approached a phone in the lobby of my hotel. I extracted Miguelito's phone number from my bag, wishing I had memorized it ahead of time. A guide appeared suddenly. She was a pretty young woman, like most of the guides, and she nearly fell as she raced across the lobby to intercept my effort to make a call. As she reached for the slip of paper I held in one hand, she urged me, in a bubbly voice, to allow her to help me with the call. "This is Cuba, the workers' paradise," she said. "Everything is different here. Our phones are different," she insisted. "Our coins are different, and so is our system of phone numbers. You will need help." She smiled as she tried to seize the slip of paper.

I felt myself growing angry. What right did she have to interfere with a private phone call? I declined her offer politely, and stuffed the paper back inside my bag, zipping it shut.

After that, every time I tried to use a phone, the guide would be there, trying to find out what number I was calling.

I gave up on phone calls, and went out to the highway to find a taxi. Within seconds, a Tourist-Taxi picked me up, and I named Miguelito's street, realizing I would just have to show up unannounced, hoping that Miguelito would be home.

As we drove through a tunnel under the Bay, I wondered whether Miguelito would turn out to be content in the workers' paradise. Perhaps he would regard me as an unwelcome intruder, a *Yanqui* Imperialist. Perhaps he would think of me as a worm, a *gusano* , the derogatory name Cuban Revolutionaries applied to those who chose exile. During my last visit, in 1960, I had been out playing in the streets of Havana with Miguelito and my other cousins and a few of the neighborhood street children, when a roving band of propagandists came by with megaphones, announcing that the *Yanquis* had canceled Cuba's quota for sugar exports to the U.S. and that, in retaliation, Cuba was preparing to nationalize all U.S. enterprises including sugar mills, oil refineries, and the North American-owned utilities, telephone and telegraph companies. I listened to the announcements indifferently. I was eight years old at the time, and cared little for the battles of the adults. I was much more interested in the mysterious activities of the children, who came and went as they pleased, disappearing into the labyrinth of Havana with their knives and their daring nicknames, reminding me of so many who did the same in my own neighborhood in Spanish Harlem.

One of the children ran to meet the propagandists, whispering to the announcers that in their midst was an innocent *Yanqui*-born child who might be offended by the names they were calling us.

The announcers swiftly altered their message, explaining that the Cuban people bore no ill will against the *Yanqui* people, but only against their government, which had been exploiting Cuba since the turn of the century and which continued to act as if it believed it could control the island just because Cuba was small.

Perplexed, I thanked my street friend but I didn't understand why he'd thought I would be offended. What did any government have to do with me? I didn't care who owned the sugar mills, and couldn't imagine that I would ever care what happened between the two governments. Both, in my opinion, had been acting stubbornly, and I didn't expect them to change. They would go on bullying each other, until sooner or later they both ended up getting hurt or getting in trouble.

Miguelito was too young at the time to understand any of it. He observed me from a distance, grimacing when I picked up small wild creatures in the park near his house, acting as if he thought I was the strangest girl he'd ever seen, one who would rather play with lizards and insects than with dolls.

Now, as the taxi approached his street, I lost my fear of being followed and gave the driver Miguelito's address, saying that I was a friend of a friend who'd been asked to deliver greetings and some little gifts. I had been in Cuba less than a day and already I was lying.

———— ᴄᴎᴐ ————

On the morning of his arrest, Gabriel journeyed from the corral to the gate of the green pasture, just as he always did. There, he whistled at his sister Amparo's fine red mare and its copper-hued colt, which Amparo had given to her half-Yanqui granddaughter, who left after an extended visit on the farm. That girl had loved the farm the way Gabriel himself did, the way his mother did, as a gift from God, a miracle of creation. Every millimeter of this red sugar land was miraculous–the pasture grasses, the hard sweet cane, the fragrant guava thickets, the papaya, mango, mamey, anón, guanábana and mamonsillo trees, the feathery leaves and hidden starchy tubers of the yuca, the big dark glossy heart-shaped leaves and buried brown tubers of the malanga, the cattle, horses, pigs, chickens, guinea hens, even the wild creatures, the black circling vultures, the turtles, jutías, iguanas, boa constrictors, tarantulas, scorpions, chanting bull frogs, singing tree frogs, the raucous flocks of wild green parrots with their painted faces, the small shiny irridescent black totí birds, the elegant striped tocororos, the great variety of tiny, brilliantly colored songbirds, and the creatures of the river–sea turtles, manatees, sharks–wandering upstream from the sea until they reached water too fresh to sustain them.

Gabriel chuckled, remembering how surprised Amparo had been when her granddaughter chose to stay on the farm instead of in Trinidad or Havana. How Amparo had gone on about the girl's strange attachment to the land! Amparo had always hated the farm. Her fear of wild creatures was absolute, especially frogs. Amparo, Miguel, Daniel, Isabelita, all of Gabriel's twelve brothers and sisters had moved to town sooner or later and some of them had even moved on, to Havana or to other distant cities, taking up professions in the arts mostly which their parents would never have dreamed of, as if they had not all been born peasants, guajiros, as if they didn't care for the sweep of green hills with its thatched bohío huts and untamed cattle, as if they didn't care for the farm traversed by red trails which resembled veins.

Each person has his own obsession, Gabriel had concluded: Amparo her love for the comforts and safety of town, Miguel his ballerinas and music, Daniel his historical studies, Isabelita her paintings.

How glad Amparo had been when they'd managed to get the child off the island before the situation grew any worse. Yanquis weren't welcome anymore, not even those who were half-Cuban. Amparo said the lines to get someone out were very long, winding away from the embassies, all the way through Havana, like serpents; and crowds of revolutionaries would follow the lines shouting gusano, shouting worm, parasite, vermin, saying how dare you leave now when the revolution needs your faith. Of course the angry ones had no way of knowing the child didn't belong here, hadn't been born here, was only half-Cuban. And what if they hadn't managed to get her out? What would have become of her, stranded on the island just when things were getting out of control again, just when everyone was starting to realize that the victory of Fidel's Barbudo rebels might not mean an end to all the turmoil after all.

Gabriel remembered how often his wife had asked the girl why she didn't care for the things she could have so easily in the North—pretty dresses and dolls, jewelry, hair ribbons. The girl hadn't seemed to understand it herself. It was just an instinct some people were born with, a love of the land, a calling, like the calling to be a priest or a nun, something you just had to answer if that passion was given to you as a gift.

Don't go out barefoot, Amparo had warned her, there are tiny invisible worms in the mud that can crawl in through the soles of your feet and climb up inside you and eat you from the inside out. Don't play with the tarantulas, they bite. Don't touch the scorpions, they're poisonous, they'll make your mouth puff up and your throat will swell shut so you can't breathe. Stop trying to pet the vultures, they're filthy. Don't ride too fast, don't get near the bull, don't copy Gabriel and his boys when they curse, don't keep asking him what those words mean. Don't scratch your mosquito bites. Check your legs for ticks every evening.

Gabriel remembered his sister's warnings to the Yanqui child, the girl saying yes, yes, yes, and then going about her wildness just the same as always, ignoring everybody, acting as if she was just another one of the free creatures of the land and nobody could tell her what to do; riding too fast and falling off, getting too close to the bull, trying to chop cane with a machete even though she was told not to touch it, that it was dangerous.

The girl had kept wandering about barefoot, saying she enjoyed the feel of the mud between her toes, asking how anything as pretty as this bright red mud hurt you anyway?

So Gabriel had started taking her out every evening to show her the sunset and tell her about the land, saying, if you like it here so much then you should know what it's really like. Sometimes the sky would be full of rumbling black clouds that looked like herds of wild horses, and Gabriel would tell his niece that the lightning was so close it could strike them down any second, just the way it had killed one of his uncles and one of his white horses. That's how dangerous it is around here, Gabriel had said, preparing to tell the girl she would have to go home soon because even though the war was supposed to be over, now the Maximum Leader was announcing that he planned to crack down on banditry in the foothills of the Escambray mountains, and that could mean anything, banditry was a term leaders used whenever they didn't want you to know exactly what they meant.

Gabriel remembered how the girl had stood there under the sunset with its wild-horse clouds, gnats collecting around her eyes, mosquitoes coating her arms, and she'd just kept saying, no, uncle, please let me stay here, you don't know what it's like in the city, there are no trees, no grass, no animals, no room, uncle Gabriel, there's no room for me there. I'm surplus. There are already too many people there, uncle, they don't need one more, over there I'm just something extra, and anyway, I could help you here, I can do the milking every morning, I don't need to go to school, you can teach me to make up poems the way you do; listen, I can already do it a little bit. And then the girl started reciting verses she'd made up, only the whole purpose of poetry had escaped her, she chose small topics, birds, butterflies, tree frogs; she didn't understand it was supposed to be about the big things, the sweep of green hills, the graceful skirts of the royal palms dancing and twirling in hurricane winds, the big forested mountains, the broad sky, about noble things—honor, dignity, integrity, liberty, equality, fraternity.

Maybe children couldn't understand, especially not a Yanqui child. Maybe children didn't understand that already some of the guajiros were fighting again, hiding up there in those mountains, taking their hunting rifles and machetes, even shards of metal wrested from their wives' black iron cooking kettles, sharpened and filed into makeshift knives.

Maybe the children still didn't understand, Gabriel thought, looking back toward the thatched bohío where his grandchildren would still be asleep, where even his wife might not yet realize that the rumors could be true, yes, they really could be surrounded by troops now.

"You look more Cuban than Yanqui," said the cabdriver as he turned to inspect me. I wished I had found a taxi farther away from the hotel. This driver seemed too interested in my activities. I had been warned that taxi drivers were often members of the Communist Party, men whose careers advanced by turning people in to the secret police for any suspicious movements or statements. I didn't want to keep lying but I had entered Cuba disguised as a tourist, and now I would have to continue pretending.

I laughed and said, "Really?" treating his comment as a joke. As we arrived at Miguelito's familiar house, I looked up at the crumbling stone and peeling white paint faded to gray. I looked across at the park with its big trees and at the sea beyond, the harbor nearly inactive now that Soviet and East German ships were no longer arriving. I felt like a person in a dream, seeing things remembered from some other era of existence, wondering which was real, the dream or the memory.

I paid the driver and told him not to wait, I would be visiting for at least an hour. He left with a friendly wave and I decided perhaps my sense of being followed and watched was paranoia from seeing too many spy movies about communist countries. But uncle Juan had told me not to trust anybody in Cuba, not even family, and my grandmother Amparo had told me she was afraid I could be arrested the minute I stepped off the plane just because I was a relative of Gabriel's.

I walked up a series of old marble steps to Miguelito's heavy wooden door. Nothing had changed. The house was still here, although peeling and crumbling. The park was still green and graceful, the sea still sparkling, the sky still blue streaked with black storm clouds. The air was hot and moist, scented by *alelí* and Madagascar jasmine. I hesitated at the door, suddenly feeling ridiculous showing up after so many years to meet a cousin I hadn't seen since he was four, intending to tell him he wasn't forgotten.

Why should he believe me and, what's more, why should he care? In the U.S., such a visit would be unimaginable.

I knocked and waited, my anticipation slipping away as the wooden door remained shut. Relief and disappointment combined as I decided that my cousin was probably away on vacation or at work, or perhaps he had moved without informing relatives in the U.S.

I knocked again just to be sure and waited again. I was just about to turn away, telling myself at least I had tried, when the door creaked slightly open and a face peered out. A tall, slender man looked down at me. He was handsome, with a full dark moustache that gave him the appearance of a cowboy in a movie about the American West. He looked like he should be wearing chaps and spurs.

He leaned down toward me, and for a few seconds we were both silent as I tried to figure out how to introduce myself. His serious expression suddenly gave way to a youthful smile, and he reached out from behind the door to embrace me with one arm.

"I know who you are!" he said softly, shaking an index finger the way people do when they say, "Aha!"

Delighted that he could recognize me after thirty-one years, I laughed, and followed him as he led me behind the wooden door and up another marble staircase inside the house.

"They divided the house and gave the rest to other families," he explained as we climbed. The house, by North American standards, would not be considered large, but it had once been very elegant, one of the homes built to house colonial Spanish gentry long before the island gained its independence.

We reached the top story, and I realized that this house which, in the old Cuba, might have harbored many branches of the same family, now held several unrelated families, like apartment buildings in the U.S.

Miguelito ushered me into a familiar many-windowed room wrapped in sunlight and furnished with hand-carved mahogany from the precious-wood forests which had once covered the island. My cousin led me to a big rocking chair in front of a window which faced the park. He sat me down in front of a portrait of my great-grandmother, my grandmother Amparo's mother, the mother of my great uncle Gabriel and of Miguelito's own father, Miguel. The portrait looked out across the park as if the old woman's image could enjoy looking at swaying trees and the sea beyond. In front of the portrait stood a small altar with flowers, candles and an image of Cuba's patron Saint, *La Virgen de la Caridad del Cobre*, Our Lady of Charity of Cobre.

I sat alone with the memory of my great-grandmother while Miguelito vanished down a dark hallway. This interval gave me a chance to enjoy my journey into the past, my sense of encountering the familiar unharmed–the park, the sea, the house, the portrait, my cousin.

Miguelito returned leading his mother. She was now stooped and very old. She was one of the thinnest women I had ever seen, so frail it seemed a careless touch could shatter her into countless pieces of fine crystal. I remembered her as a beautiful woman, gracious, the descendant of wealthy Spaniards, a woman who had stepped into an unfamiliar realm when she married my great-uncle Miguel, the son of rugged *guajiros*, still chopping their own cane and milking their own cows on a remote sweep of green hills far away from the elegance of Havana.

Miguelito's mother walked holding onto her son with one hand and to the peeling wall with the other.

"My mother," said Miguelito. "She's afraid of walking, afraid she'll fall." He had noticed that I was wondering why she held onto the wall. "The government," he then added, "does not believe in paint." Again he had read my thoughts.

"The whole city is falling down," he said. "Everything is peeling and crumbling: the paint, the stone, the statues. Houses are collapsing while people still live in them. But what can you do? You can't move. No one moves in Cuba, unless they can find someone who wants to trade houses. We're not allowed to sell our house or buy a new one, and there's no paint or plaster or any kind of materials to fix anything."

He led his mother to another rocking chair facing mine. Then he found one for himself and, looking around the room, I realized that rocking chairs were the only seats available. They were scattered all over the room, big, imposing rocking chairs. As a child I had always loved hammocks and rocking chairs. I had associated them with stability, with relaxation, patience, a dreamy state of mind found only in the very young and very old.

Miguelito turned to his mother and explained, "This is Amparo's granddaughter. She came from over there to see us." The old woman studied me, her memory struggling. "Aah," she finally sighed. "From the other side." She smiled at me, and added, "People used to do that, you know, go to the other side for awhile and come back. Now they never come back."

Understanding that she meant exiled family members never returned to Cuba anymore, I nodded and said, "Perhaps someday they will again." I offered her a piece of strawberry candy wrapped in red foil with the ends twisted like Chinese fans. She took it and held it until her son explained what it was, unwrapping the candy for her and showing her that the foil could be discarded.

"Aah," she repeated, "*caramelitos*, I remember them."

Miguelito tilted his head slightly in a gesture that indicated patience, and told me, "Things like this, candies, small things, here they don't exist anymore."

I smiled in sympathy. "Nothing inside this room has changed," I said, "the view, the way the sun comes in these windows." I found the view exhilarating, the room light and airy, the company of people I hadn't seen for so long enchanting. I felt like a child again, fascinated by every detail of my surroundings.

Miguelito stood abruptly and flung the windows wide open, one at a time, in a ceremonial manner. Still facing the windows, he stood absorbing the sea breeze and announced in a loud voice, "This is my house, and I will say whatever I want to say. I don't care if they take me away to the prison camps, because what do I have left to lose?"

He turned to face me. He seemed very tall and dignified, proud. "What do I have left to lose?" he asked, and suddenly his shoulders slumped and he moved away from the window. Seated once again, he leaned close to me and said, "Look, you came out of an airplane, right? But you might as well have come out of a spaceship, walking upside down." He used the fingers of one hand to illustrate how space creatures might walk, legs pointed up instead of down.

His gaze searched my face for understanding. I nodded. "That," he said, "is how different your life has been from mine."

For a moment I was afraid he was angry with me, but soon he smiled and I saw that his bitterness was not against those who had escaped to outer space.

"We have a son," he said cheerfully. Then he left me with his mother and, disappearing down the dark hallway, he went to fetch his wife and child. I sat alone with the old woman, saying nothing, the two of us rocking and looking out the window, remembering.

When Miguelito returned with his wife, she embraced me and introduced their child who, like my cousin and my great-uncle Miguel, was already very tall.

"Do you know how we recognized you?" my cousin's wife asked, grinning. She was very beautiful and wonderfully warm. I felt myself enveloped by peace, the hot fragrant air, the breeze coming in through open windows, the return to a reality I had feared might no longer exist, the recognition.

"Aurora," Miguelito urged, "show her the picture." His wife left to find a box of photographs, and she came back holding one that Amparo had sent of my wedding day, a younger version of myself smiling and holding a bouquet of orange blossoms and roses, my North American husband smiling at my side.

"What I remember about you," Miguelito said, shaking a finger as if to scold me, "is the way you liked to play with spiders and lizards." He grimaced and shuddered in an exaggerated manner, just as he had when he was little. "You caught those huge terrible spiders," he said, revealing that he was a true city dweller, still afraid of tarantulas. "And you would carry them around in your hand!"

His wife also made a face indicating disgust.

"I still prefer the countryside," I laughed, explaining that in some ways I hadn't changed much.

"¡Qué horror!" Miguelito responded, still picturing me playing with tarantulas, not realizing that to me the real horrors were in the city: gray sky, the odor of fumes, mile after mile of paved streets with no trees to dance when a breeze came along, and the junkies, pimps and gangs, and the curling smoke of my opium, laced with dreams of dragons and mermaids, gargoyles and sirens.

Yet I understood my cousin's childhood fear of spiders because I had also been frightened by a beast in Cuba. It happened before Miguelito's birth, when I was only two, and we were on the island visiting my grandmother and all her family in Havana and Trinidad.

It was the summer of 1953, when Fidel Castro had launched his first attack against the forces of Batista. The attack failed and Castro was arrested, but later he was released and went into exile in Mexico, returning on a small boat with a band of *guerrilla* warriors who landed near the eastern mountains of Oriente province. This time they fought until they succeeded in deposing the tyrant hated by peasants like Gabriel.

The beast which terrified me while Fidel was attacking Moncada was an enormous anaconda at the Havana Zoo. I was walking hand in hand with my *Abuelita* Amparo, and beside her were her brothers Miguel and Daniel. Gabriel was on his farm, and Isabelita was in Trinidad painting rural Cuban landscapes and portraits of my great-grandmother.

When we passed the anaconda's cage the adults were talking and laughing. No one else seemed to notice the great serpent's hunger. I stopped, and met the snake's greedy stare, certain that the beast intended to consume me. Too young to speak or think, I stood transfixed by terror. That moment became frozen in time and was lost deep within my memory until many years later when it emerged, along with other trapped memories and visions of demons.

Now, facing Miguelito as he reminded me how frightened he had been when he saw me exploring Cuba's soil for small wild creatures, I wondered whether, during all the years of separation, he had thought of me only when he thought of gruesome beasts.

I pulled out a bag filled with candy, each wrapper decorated with the image of some colorful northern fruit, strawberries, apples, peaches. Miguelito, Aurora and the old women all stared hard at the mound of candies, at the fishtails of twisted foil, the inside of each wrapper silvery like fish scales. I poured the candies out of the bag onto a dish Miguelito held out to catch them. He and his wife exchanged glances, shaking their heads as if they had seen something wondrous.

They passed the dish of candy around, admiring the colors and gleam. Aurora said she wanted to show them to her friends. Only the old lady tasted the sweets. I brought out all the other gifts sent by exiled relatives, the soaps, T-shirts, diapers, baseball caps, spools of thread, safety pins, flashlights, calculators, canned sausage, coffee, chewing gum.

Miguelito sniffed at a package of gum. "It's been a long time," he said softly. Aurora smelled the soaps, and said, "It's these little things we forget here, smells, tastes, designs, details." Little, I thought, but perhaps not insignificant.

"And choices," my cousin added. "Sometimes I think what would it be like to have a choice. Tell me, for instance, is it true your husband can walk into a big store full of beer and choose from several different kinds, any kind he wants, and each one will taste different?"

I nodded. "Dozens of kinds. Maybe hundreds."

"And which does he like best?" Miguelito asked, looking like a child caught up in a fantasy world, imagining something too beautiful to be true, a world of unicorns and dragons, leprechauns and wishes granted by magic.

I tried to remember which brands my husband asked for when I went grocery shopping. "Coors," I said, "or Millers and imported kinds too, I guess, Corona." I remembered all the odd brands he'd tried on occasion, names like Moosehead, or beers from exotic places like Singapore and Ceylon, with decorative labels that looked like pages out of a National Geographic magazine.

"Here," my cousin told me, "we have one kind of beer only. It comes in a brown bottle with no label, government beer, produced by the State. I would be very curious to taste different flavors. This year," he continued, "there is plenty of beer and ice cream but little else. They give us beer to make up for all the food shortages, and to try to make up for canceling carnival on account of the economic crisis."

In Cuba, there had once been many saints' day carnivals, as well as the one before Lent. Now the main carnival was supposed to commemorate Revolution Day, July 26, the anniversary of Fidel's attack on the Moncada Barracks during the summer of 1953.

I looked out at the hot sky with its black clouds.

"It is very unlikely," my cousin said wistfully, "that they would ever let me travel. I knew he meant the government when he said "they". In New York, Amparo and Juan always said "they" when referring to the Cuban government.

Miguelito shook his head. "No," he repeated, "I am considered a dissident. Quiet, but a dissident. I would not be allowed to travel."

When he asked, I told Miguelito that yes, I had traveled a great deal, leaving behind a turbulent New York childhood, abandoning opium dreams, dragons and mermaids. I told him, even though I could see his envy, that yes, freedom was tangible, once you had known it you could keep it with you, carry it inside, treasure it even if you had to keep it secret.

Now, as my cousin stepped to the window of the house he'd lived in since birth, under the watchful eye of my great-grandmother's portrait, I felt a great tenderness for him, for his wife and child, and for his mother with her mercifully fading memory.

Aurora rose from her rocking chair and began closing windows. She looked nervous, anxious. Miguelito reached out to stop her hand. "Leave them open," he commanded. His mother looked up at him mournfully. Both women retreated, disappearing down the dark hallway, taking the child with them, holding onto the walls as they walked. Before vanishing into the hallway, Aurora turned to me and whispered, "What will become of us?"

"I want to know about freedom, but I am a quiet dissident," Miguelito offered, watching me intently. He looked so much like a cowboy in a Western movie that I expected him to whip out a gun and start shooting out the windows, over the fluttering skirts of the trees in the park, toward the black Cuban storm clouds which had always reminded me of wild horses.

"Here," he said, "everything is hypocrisy. I have to be very careful. I want to write songs. I want to sing. A simpler freedom than travel, simpler than having choices. But here it is impossible. It is too dangerous. No one can write unless they belong to the Writers Union. To belong to the Writers Union you must be selected by the government. You must write what they want you to write. Painting is the same, and dance, and drama. Songwriting. Everything is controlled. You have heard the term totalitarianism, right? I know they tell you that about us over there. You've heard about communists acting like robots, doing what they're told to do, saying what they're told to say." He imitated the stiff, mechanical movements of a cartoon robot. "Well, it's true, it's all true. Everything you've ever heard about us, it's true. That's what it's like here, total power for one man, total. And I know you must wonder, so I'm telling you. Because if I was from over there, I would wonder. I would want you to tell me, I would expect you to confide.

"This," my cousin continued, "is a poem the children memorize in school, 'Fidel is always present...as if his boots had wings'. "

The words of the poem would have been lovely if the subject had been God or the angels. I felt terribly saddened for my cousin who wanted to write songs but could not, would not, without endangering his family by crossing the line from quiet dissident to prohibited voice.

"He treats us," my cousin said, gazing upward toward the crumbling ceiling, choosing his words carefully, "like children. Every little thing is decided for us, what we will study, where we will work, where we will live, where we will go on vacation, what we will eat for dinner."

Miguelito extracted a booklet from his pocket and handed it to me, flipping the pages to show me a series of entries on small rectangles of lined paper. "This is the only way I have ever in my entire life obtained food," he said. "I am only a little older than the revolution. So you see, since I was a very small child, this is all I have ever known. He was looking out the window again, speaking in a loud voice. I don't enjoy the career they chose for me. It is technical work, productive, it has value, but it's not what I want to do. I feel paralyzed, strangled."

My mind was racing with empathy and new perceptions. My cousin had said he didn't care if he went to the prison camps, but he also said he had to be careful for his family's sake. He said there was nothing left to lose, yet here he was living in a portion of his father's house with a wife, child and an aging mother who needed him. So perhaps he was referring to the intangibles he had already lost: honor, dignity and integrity, liberty, equality and fraternity, all the noble, poetic promises represented on the island's coat of arms.

"Come," my cousin commanded. To me he seemed to have plenty of honor and dignity as he led me down the dark hallway. Integrity too, because here he was speaking openly about forbidden topics. The presence of an outsider, a foreigner, seemed to have loosened a flood of words he had been restraining around Cubans. I knew about Neighborhood Committees for the Defense of the Revolution because I read my human rights bulletins faithfully and because Amparo and Juan had told me what it was like to be watched by the neighbors, to be turned in to the secret police for any little complaint or for unauthorized gatherings of more than seven people meeting in a house or for possession of more butter than your ration coupons entitled you to buy.

I hoped Miguelito would close the windows next time he wanted to confide his longing for simple freedoms such as traveling or composing new songs. If my presence was going to hurl open a floodgate of honesty, I wanted to make sure we weren't overheard by suspicious neighbors.

Halfway down the hall, Miguelito stopped and pointed out a framed photograph of my mother when she was young and pregnant. "So you see," my cousin said, "you've been here in Cuba all along, hanging on the wall, waiting to be born."

Then he led me into a room with small high windows and old mahogany furniture. Carvings on the wood depicted peacocks, angels, cherubs, roses, palm trees. I had the impression I was in the depths of a forest, surrounded by dancers, hearing drums and wailing lyrics, praise and lamentations.

My cousin took me by the elbow. I could hear his wife reading to their son in another room. I was frightened, not by my cousin, but by the shadowy forests of the room, haunted by music and ballerinas, torn by a flurry of wings and fangs. Graceful palms, pale dancers, hills, horses and cattle, vultures, parrots, all were here: as were sky, sun, pastures, fields of sugarcane.

"This," my cousin told me, still holding onto my elbow in a protective gesture, "is the room where my father killed himself just a few months ago."

I knew Miguel had died recently but I didn't know that his death had been a suicide. The battling of wings and fangs was intense now. The music was deafening. I wondered if Miguelito was aware of the angels and demons in this room, the ambushes, attacks, struggles, the singing and hissing.

Gradually, the feeling of being trapped passed, but the angels and demons still surrounded us. I could see some of the demons, and I could hear the singing of angels. The room was still dark and mysterious, still a wilderness of primitive jungle and savage farm. I was beginning to feel at home in this room. Everything was familiar, the visions, the music, the wind.

Miguelito drew me over to one side of the room, under a high window guarded by a large crucifix. "Right here," he said, "is where my father killed himself. I knew he was going to do it because he told me. He was old and sick, and he was discouraged. He knew he wasn't getting better, nothing was getting better, and something in his spirit was already dead. The suffering was too much for him. So he took a clean white cloth and wrapped it around his neck and tied it to the window, there, and strangled himself."

I remembered Miguel as a brilliant singer and dancer, a man who with his voice could bring to life mountains, islands, the sea. I remembered how triumphant Miguel had felt after the revolution was over, when truckloads of bearded troops were roaming Havana, cheered by jubilant crowds. During the summer of 1960, the songs of my great-uncle Miguel had been like floating balloons filled with hope, songs promising liberty and justice.

Miguelito now picked up a guitar with broken strings, and began to sing his father's words. Then he leaned the guitar against a wall, and continued speaking. "I came into this room and found him dead."

A wing bumped me, and I moved across the room, gazing into the walls, seeing scenes from Miguel's childhood on the farm which once belonged to his parents and later to Gabriel. I thought of the legendary Cuban troubadours who had risked their lives by walking the streets of Havana during the early 1930's, singing protest songs during a student rebellion against the hated dictator Machado.

Miguel had been one of those singers, and his songs had been an inspiration to the rebels, among them his brother Daniel, who had also moved to Havana as a young man, and was one of the university students leading the rebellion. I remembered how Miguel had once told me that Machado's secret police tried to shoot him down for singing on the streets. He had laughed, saying "But now here I am, doing the same for another revolution, against another tyrant, and now we've won, and no one can ever tell me to stop singing." But he'd been wrong. They had told him to stop.

Scattered throughout the haunted room, angels whispered and demons shrieked.

Miguelito was silent for a long moment. Then he startled me by asking, "And you, have you ever considered suicide?"

Yes, it was true, Miguelito and I were very much alike. I nodded. All around me, dancers twirled embraced by royal palms. The ghostly white legs of the dancers were luminescent, showered by moonlight. The trees accompanying them pirouetted. We were in the mountains, in a village hidden by jungle.

"Yes," I answered, "I did consider suicide, I considered it seriously." I was thinking of my youth in Spanish Harlem, of the opium dreams, the dragons and sirens.

"Aah," my cousin said, "you see." And somehow I felt certain that his response was one of recognition, an awareness of our similarity.

Miguelito closed his eyes. He was listening to the music around us. I began to realize that not all of the songs in this room were coming from angels or from my great-uncle's ghost. Miguelito was also singing, his voice flowing through the hot moist air, mingling with the humming of angels and clawing of demons.

When his song ended, my cousin opened his eyes abruptly.

"I have considered suicide myself," Miguelito said, "very profoundly."

The music resumed as his confession ended.

"Sometimes," Miguelito said, speaking above the melody and rhythm of his own imagination, "I talk to God. Sometimes I ask God to help me, but here I am, still waiting, feeling that I've been forgotten."

A cloud of striped butterflies came flickering across the room. I could see cobblestone streets, a belltower, caves, flying fish, all the experiences of my great-uncle Miguel's life, traveling through the room, trapped here, like small caged songbirds caught wild in the mountains and carried into town in bamboo cages, to be hung in quiet patios, and taken out for walks at sunset.

"Yes," Miguelito repeated, "I have considered suicide."

———ᴄᴧɔ———

On the morning of Gabriel's arrest he went out into the pasture to catch his stallion, and he mounted the animal bareback, proud to be riding a descendant of Moorish steeds escaped from the stables of the Conquerors in the early 1500's, when Diego de Velásquez, commissioned by Spain as Governor-General of Hispaniola, set sail for Cuba, prepared to conquer and colonize the island .

The stallion was suited to wilderness. It was small and sturdy, with a gracefully curved neck, a mixture of caution for evading hunters and boldness for survival in a rugged land. Like my own sons and grandsons, Gabriel thought.

He trotted the horse. Then, clicking his tongue and shouting "¡Arre, caballo!" he set off cantering across his few caballerías of treasured land, as he did every morning, to assure himself that the land was still thriving and safe, a gift placed in his care.

The horse was a rodeo animal and Gabriel, a Cuban cowboy, was an expert at roping and herding. On horseback he felt exhilarated, breathing in the mingled odors of sugarcane and manure.

The stallion rolled across the land in a canter, bred for the arid hills of Spain and, before that, for the deserts of North Africa. It was a pace Gabriel could enjoy forever, the way he enjoyed rolling off one verse after another when he and his brothers and sons and cousins all got together for a duel of improvised décimas, the traditional impromptu, unwritten songs of Cuban troubadours.

The silence of the land was intense today. Gabriel found such deep silence menacing. In the wild lands it seemed unnatural. He should have been hearing the cries of birds, the calls of frogs, the braying of distant burros.

Even his humped white bull was silent today, standing alone in the fibrous green pasture. "Such a profound silence," Gabriel said to his horse, hoping to break the spell. The stallion tossed its neck, a splash of gray mane like the foam of a pale stormy sea.

Gabriel figured that with his own mixed blood of conqueror and conquered, even if the rumors were true, he would find some way of evading the troops which might come swooping down like predators. After all, guajiros were hardy folks. How many rebellions had his own mother survived? She'd been born during the Ten Years War, some time between 1868 and 1878, at a time when hardly no one could remember the exact year of a birth. During that war which lasted an entire decade, tens of thousands of Cubans died, taking with them hundreds of thousands of Spanish soldiers and, still, when it was over and the treaties had been signed, the Cubans were not really free. Spain had promised reforms, but soon the seeds of rebellion were scattered again.

Then the brief Little War came and went, and finally, beginning in 1895, three years of bloodshed, inspired by the pleas for freedom and justice of the poet José Martí. That had been the final war against Spain but, later, in the 1930's, there had been the revolution against Machado's tyranny, and then, beginning with Fidel's attack at Moncada in 1953 and ending with the Barbudos' triumphant march into Havana, there had been the glorious revolution against the despot Batista. It had seemed glorious at the time, Gabriel reflected, and certainly inside, somewhere inside, there had been a kind of glory crying out of the heart and mind.

And through it all, Gabriel's mother had never lost the family or the farm. Through it all, even after her husband died, leaving her with thirteen children to feed, she had always managed to milk the cows and grow some corn and sugarcane.

Whenever a war started, the sugar fields were set aflame, and a cry of rage would ring from the mouths of the peasants, all across the land, a cry like the bloodcurdling scream of the Cuban Mambí warriors who swept down from their hiding places in the caves and mountains to ambush Spanish troops.

Gabriel figured he was much like his horse, much like Cuba herself, part medieval Spanish Knight, with a blend of cimarrón African slave and whatever remnants of the Taíno, Siboney and Guanahacabibe Indians might have survived Diego Velásquez and his Conquerors.

Remembering all the wars and rebellions his mother had endured keeping the farm and her family intact, Gabriel brought his horse to a halt and, scanning the horizon, shook his fist at the devil, just as he always did in the morning after the milking and his daily ride.

————∽————

I wandered along mile after mile of beach, past countless hotels hastily built by order of the Maximum Leader to attract tourists to Cuba, bringing with them foreign currency and forbidden ideas. I strolled past the soldiers guarding the beaches.

I wandered along the beaches, my feet plowing through soft white sand. Cuban families were confined to separate bathing areas to prevent them from mingling with foreigners, but some of the young people waved at me from inner tubes where they loafed in the shallow water and I wondered how many of them would eventually try to float away. Some might reach Key West. Others would drown or die of thirst or be killed by sharks.

I remembered reading about a family of refugees lost at sea. They tied their raft to a sea turtle, and let the animal tow them to safety, taking the chance that it might dive and pull them into the depths.

The hotel shops were now selling stuffed sea turtles by the thousands. The heads were mounted on plaques above the coarsely painted word, CUBA. How long would it take, I wondered, before the government had no endangered animal species left to sell? The Maximum Leader had recently announced that to keep the economy going he would negotiate even with the devil.

I remembered walking along these same beaches in 1960, before the hotels were built, when the sands were still deserted and the sea held more manatees and flying fish than teenagers hoping to float away to Miami.

On those walks I had been fascinated by the soaring fish, by the yellow shells of moon snails, by red and black land crabs and the leaning trunks of coconut palms tossed by wind.

Now, a blackboard had been set out on the sand in front of one of the hotels. On its dull green surface a list had been scribbled, "Volleyball, diving, cave tour, windsurfing, authentic *guajiro guateque*. " I stopped in front of the blackboard, transfixed. *Guateque*. What memories came with that word! Gabriel and his sons inventing *décimas*, their songs, their fingers dancing on the strings of small guitars which resembled banjos, the *maracas, güiro*, and other traditional instruments; Gabriel roasting a pig in an earthen pit, his wife serving the meat with a sauce of sour orange and garlic; a crowd of cousins consuming spiced corn meal tamales wrapped in banana leaves; everyone smiling and laughing, the rapid musical voices, the dances, rope tricks, poetry duels, each man challenging the others to pull from his heart a more noble word, a more passionate verse.

I felt afflicted, cursed. How many years had Gabriel spent in prison before dying? Now this hotel, built by the Maximum Leader, dared to advertise the authentic country feasts of peasants imprisoned under the orders of *El Líder Máximo*. They were turning the *guateque* into a Caribbean version of the Hawaiian luau. They were portraying free and joyful peasants. They were deceiving the tourists.

When Abuelita Amparo tried to visit Gabriel in prison, the Instructor said he didn't exist. No such man had been arrested. There were no records documenting his detention. Perhaps he had merely been picked up for questioning? Perhaps he was still being questioned, a formality, nothing more.

Several years later, when Amparo was finally allowed to see her brother, she saw that he did exist, although in a reduced form, a much smaller man, withered by beatings, prison food and the cold cement floors. Without his farm and his freedom, Gabriel had been sucked dry like the remains of one of those caterpillars imprisoned by solitary wasps, the wasps that keep their prey paralyzed by venom in the underground caverns where they lay their eggs, the caterpillars devoured alive, slowly, by the newly hatched wasp larvae. And he, the Maximum Leader, was the poisonous wasp.

I remembered Gabriel bellowing "¡Arre, caballo!," the equivalent of "giddyap!" I didn't know whether his arrest for counter-revolutionary activity had been based on real evidence but I knew enough about the Cuban Penal Code to feel certain that there was always room for doubt, especially during the turmoil of the early 1960's.

I remembered Gabriel as a vehement Castrista, a revolutionary peasant shaking his fist at the devil, jubilant when the Barbudos triumphed over the old tyrant Batista. I thought of Gabriel as a twentieth-century knight challenging an enormous fire-breathing dragon. I thought of Gabriel as another José Martí, as a poet-patriot charging into battle on a pale horse, ready to die for the words represented by the Cuban coat-of-arms, the liberty, equality, fraternity, honor, dignity and integrity.

Of course, my thoughts of Gabriel were the thoughts of a child, and I really didn't know whether he had actually carried out some prohibited counter-revolutionary act after growing disillusioned with the new Maximum Leader.

All I really knew about Gabriel was that without his farm, he would die, in or out of prison, physically or spiritually, because the man and the land were one.

I walked away from the blackboard with its false offering of joyous feasts. The beach was melancholy now, people roaming hopelessly along the sand, floating helplessly in the shallow water, enclosed by smooth black rubber inner tubes.

Some North American scientists recently reported that sixty million years ago, a great meteor crashed into the earth, killing all the dinosaurs. The meteor is believed to have plunged into the sea at a spot near the belly of the alligator-shaped island of Cuba. The island itself may be nothing more than a ridge on the edge of a deep crater formed by the falling star, according to the geological studies.

It is a discovery Gabriel would have enjoyed. He would have liked to hear how scientists were able to decipher prehistoric heavenly events by peering closely at tiny crystals in rocks found at the bottom of the sea.

Without Gabriel, I never would have noticed the alligator shape of Cuba but once he told me about it, I could distinguish, very clearly, the long tail curving toward Yucatan, the bumpy nose pointing toward Haiti, and one eye lifted above the water, glaring at Jamaica.

Although Daniel was the one who studied history, Gabriel was always the one to tell me about the plight of the Cuban Indians. The Siboney and Guanahacabibe tribes were nomadic hunter-gatherers, who used fish bones, seashells and unpolished stones as tools. They were timid, and hid in caves to escape the Conquerors. Gabriel gave me a translucent yellow stalactite from a cave once inhabited by the Siboney.

The Taínos were more sedentary, although they still hunted and fished. The Taínos also cultivated manioc, corn, beans, squash, peanuts and tobacco, and they made tools by polishing wood and stone. They lived in thatched bamboo houses called *bohíos*, houses much like the palm-bark huts of twentiety-century Cuban *guajiros*.

Gabriel used to tell me about the Indians every evening while we watched the sunset. On farms, watching the sunset is a quiet ritual much like watching the evening news in cities. It is the perfect time to learn about people, what they're like inside, what they care about, how hopeful they feel.

Gabriel told me that the island he called enchanted is still populated by the uncounted ghosts of slaughtered Indians. When Columbus landed in Cuba, there may have been more than a hundred thousand Indians living on the island. By 1557, there were no more than two thousand. They died of slavery and disease. They were burned at the stake, fed to dogs, and disemboweled. Many of those who survived committed suicide or hid in the caves and mountains. A few of the women were married off to Spaniards and gave birth to a handful of mixed-blood Cubans who, in turn, mixed with slaves from Nigeria and the Congo, *cimarrones* who escaped and hid in the mountains, taking with them their faith in trees which could dance and people who could fly.

Gabriel said the ghosts of slaughtered Indians were believed to have survived in the form of ticks and mosquitoes determined to stay on the island tormenting the Conquistadors and all their descendants.

Gabriel told me the story of Hatuey, a Taíno chieftain who refused to be converted because he didn't want his soul to share eternity with the men who were slaughtering his people. Hatuey asked the priests whether heaven would receive *Conquistadores* and when they answered yes, of course, the defiant chieftain chose to be burned at the stake rather than accept baptism and the threat of a heaven to be shared with his tormentors.

The Conquerors searched for gold on the island but found mostly copper, marble and limestone. Because the Indians called one of the places on their island Cubanacán Columbus, hearing the word, believed he had arrived on an Asian isle and would soon meet a ruler called the Kublai Khan.

Cubanacán, it is said, means place-at-the center. The people of Cubanacán were clever fishermen and farmers. They tied small suckerfish to strings and used them to pull in bigger fish. They constructed fish traps and carved triangular stone spirit guardians called *cemís*. They buried these stone guardians in the corners of their manioc fields to protect the crops. They carved four-legged stools with concave stone seats. They carved the ribs of manatees into ceremonial spatulas which they poked down into their throats before a feast. The people of the place-at-the-center believed that the energy of lightning was transformed into stones after a storm, and that if they dug at the base of a tree struck by lightning, they would find thunderstones which could be used to heal the sick.

It was not all paradisiacal for these copper-skinned people of Cuba, Gabriel insisted. They had to contend with alligators and sharks; hurricanes swept across the island, and Carib cannibals occasionally came northwest, from Venezuela and the lesser Antilles, in big canoes, to raid for children who could be fattened for eating.

The Conquerors, thinking of themselves as lost at sea and fearful that their ships might be swallowed by sea serpents and giant octopi, were startled by the beauty of the island. Columbus wrote that Cuba was the most beautiful land human eyes had ever seen. He described mermaids and pink flamingos, flying fish and land crabs, pineapples and trees that touched the sky. He wrote that "a thousand tongues would not suffice" to tell all the marvels so wondrous and plentiful in Cuba.

Columbus tried to change the island's name to Juana, but no one paid attention. Then he tried calling the island Fernandina, but still the people kept saying Cuba. All that survived of the myriad Cuban Indians were the indigenous names and the native customs of sleeping in hammocks and smoking cigars, and a sprinkling of Taíno-blood in *guajiros* like Gabriel.

Walking along the soft sand of this tropical beach with its floating trail of melancholy bathers and my memories of Gabriel and his tales at sunset, I retained an image of thousands of Cuban Indian suicides hanging from trees, and of myself growing up in Spanish Harlem, much more *Yanqui* than Cuban, searching for guardian spirits among the street signs and telephone poles of the city.

During the Cuban Missile Crisis I was suspended for lying to a junior high school teacher about my great-uncle Gabriel. The class assignment was an essay about the best meal of our short lives. We were expected to come up with a Thanksgiving turkey or a Christmas ham. Instead, I wrote about Gabriel and his farm, about pigs and *yuca* roasted in crimson earth, about poetry duels and rope tricks, and bold, defiant men who still rode horses descended from the *cimarrón* steeds escaped from the stables of *Conquistadores*. I said there were mermaids in the river and angels in the sky, and a devil roaming the hills. I said that if you shook your fist at him often enough, the devil would leave you alone. I used words like *caballerías* and leagues, and the English teacher sent me to the vice-principal's office to be suspended for mocking a serious assignment with invented tales she claimed I'd copied from books on medieval history.

Later, uncle Juan asked me if I got the mermaids and angels from my imagination or the opium he kept telling me I shouldn't smoke, but I answered no. I remembered them from Cuba.

On the morning of Gabriel's arrest, after he slowed his stallion, shook his fist at the devil and prayed, his thoughts rested briefly on his nephews Omar, Emilio and Adán, all sons of one of Gabriel's late sisters, all rumored to be Alzados now, hiding out up in the mountains again, fighting against the Castrista forces, just as they had fought on Fidel Castro's side against the old tyrant only eighteen months earlier. The youngest would be eighteen now, the oldest twenty-three. When they began with Fidel and Che they were just children. And to think their brother Alvaro was still one of Fidel's officers, and he would be expected to hunt them down and shoot them, his own brothers.

What if it was true that Fidel was going to sell Cuba away to the Russians, after the guajiros fought so hard to keep the island free, first from Spain, later from Machado, then Batista, and now? If the rumors about Communism were true, then there would be nationalization of mid-sized farms, collectivization of small farms. Gabriel wished his brother Daniel would come visiting and explain it all to him.

Once, when sugar prices plummeted, Gabriel's father went out riding a white gelding, searching for something his family could eat, anything at all. At that time there were not yet any cattle or pigs on the farm, and all the chickens had been devoured. There was only the sugar and the wild fruit, and Gabriel and his twelve hungry brothers and sisters had finished off the last of the yuca and fruit, even the last wild guava, a fruit which always bore in such abundance that no one had ever imagined the supply could be depleted.

His father left promising to find something edible, a jutía, iguana or wild pig. Gabriel, who was still small then, had looked anxiously at his mother and had seen tears in her eyes. He had never imagined that she might cry like other people. He had always thought of her as part of the farm itself, like the white horse and the pastures and sunset. She had been the first to think of calling the farm by a name, an Indian name hardly anyone else could understand, the name of a beautiful rare songbird from the mountains, a bird so timid that hardly anyone had ever seen it alive. Hunters occasionally came down out of the mountains with feathers to sell to town women who liked to decorate their hats, and once in a very great while, the feathers would be those of the rarest and most beautiful bird in all of Cuba, and the body of the small bird would already have been eaten by then, and everyone would say they imagined a bird so glorious must have had a very sweet song when it was alive, but no one could remember hearing it sing.

Gabriel remembered the exultation he'd felt when he saw his father returning on the white horse, carrying something big and heavy in a cloth sack slung across the horse's back. The entire day had passed with all thirteen children debating the likelihood of eating that night. Gabriel remembered how their dog ran ahead of the children to meet their father, the dog barking, the children shrieking.

When the horse was released and the sack opened, out fell an enormous sea turtle, big enough to feed the family for weeks. What celebration there had been! Gabriel's father hung the turtle upside down from a ceiba branch, until its head came out of its shell. Then he lopped off the head with his shiny machete and by dusk they were all guzzling turtle soup, their mother warning them to watch their manners.

I walked into one of the hotel restaurants, and sat down in a two-story chamber made up almost entirely of glass walls and open windows. I chose a small round table draped with a white tablecloth. Cloth napkins had been folded into the shapes of seashells. At the center of the table there was a single orange, with the stem of a red hibiscus blossom resting inside a tiny hole someone had punched into the top of the fruit to make it serve as a vase. A man wearing an embroidered white *guayabera* shirt approached me, smiling and reciting the lines he'd been assigned to use on tourists. "Peace," he said. "Love." Then he gestured toward an immense buffet spread across a series of eight adjacent rectangular tables. Silver platters were heaped with yellow, red and green bananas, carved pineapples, sliced mangos, and halved guavas. Other plates held mounds of roast pork, stewed chicken, fried fish, spiced ground beef, potatoes, rice, black beans, fresh bread, cheese, and candied tropical fruits. Ice chests were filled with an assortment of imported black-market soft drinks and bottled beers, each with its own decorative label. There were bottles of rum, boxes of Cuban cigars, and half a dozen servants dressed entirely in colonial white.

I looked up at my smiling host in his white *guayabera*, thinking how little peace and love the islanders had these days, thinking of Miguel hanging himself and of Miguelito bursting with unsung words, of Aurora waiting in the ration lines, hoping her turn came before they announced that they'd run out of bread. "No more today," the distributors would say, and word would be passed down the line, a rustling sound followed by a deep communal moan. "Come back tomorrow," the distributor would command, and at the end of the line, secret police and uniformed soldiers would join forces to make sure the crowd left quietly.

On my first day in Havana I had seen this happen. The groan of disappointment was heavy, rippled, tangible. The air felt bitter, like the taste of a bad grapefruit. A guide had noticed me watching the disappointed crowd, and she had approached me and said, "The lines hardly ever run out of food. We have economic problems, but serious shortages do not exist."

Now I looked from my smiling white-shrouded host to the pile of food on the hotel buffet tables, wondering how long it would be until the Cuban people rebelled against the man who was selling their food to foreigners.

I abruptly lost my appetite, not because the food was stolen from the mouths of the people by the man who claimed to be their liberator, but because the hypocrisy of my host's smile sickened me. Yet I knew he had no choice if he wanted to survive on this bewitched island without risking his own safety and that of his family. In Cuba there seemed to be only three choices, tyranny, rebellion or escape. Nothing had changed since the days of the *Conquistadores*, the slaughtered Indians, the African slaves.

I nodded at the host, trying to smile, and said, yes, I would serve myself shortly. He bowed and moved away to stand protectively next to the mountain of stolen food.

I planned to sit quietly, thinking about Miguelito's dilemma.

A black streak suddenly shot across the wide restaurant, hitting one of the glass walls and plunging to the floor.

A scream rose from somewhere below, reverberating against the glass walls. I stood and saw below me, at the bottom of a marble staircase, a maid holding her mop.

"A little bird has killed itself!" she shrieked. She ran to lift the small, irridescent black form of a *totí* which had, apparently, flown through the open windows and crashed into a glass wall. The maid rushed to a faucet, holding the inert bird. She turned on the cold water full blast, and held the creature under a powerful stream, spreading its wings out as if by doing so she could make it fly.

The white-clad cooks, waiters and hosts all came forward to watch as the maid tried to bring this small shiny bird back to life. After rinsing it thoroughly, she took it outside and set it down on the tiles of an open-air dance floor which overlooked the sea. I followed. The bird lay flat on its side, showing no signs of life.

Everyone turned away, the men shrugging, the maid sobbing quietly. I went back into the glass room and served myself a generous buffet of all the foods my Cuban cousins were not allowed to eat. I had asked Miguelito and Amparo whether I could invite them to a tourist restaurant but my cousin had said no, it could cause serious problems. They weren't supposed to speak to foreigners and since I didn't have the proper permits for visiting them as a relative, even an outing to a restaurant could place them in the position of appearing to seek forbidden contact with outsiders. It all seemed so irrational to me that I thought I might be imagining the list of absurd rules.

Feeling a new surge of appetite, I finished my feast, then filled my bag with bread, cheese and candied fruit. I descended the marble staircase and emerged again, onto the tiles of the dance floor. As I stepped into the brilliant sunlight, I saw that the wounded bird was gone. It had only been stunned, and had now recovered and flown away. I felt tremendously relieved, as if the fate of the bird were somehow attached to the fate of my suicidal cousin.

That night I slept soundly in my hotel room, a sleep devoid of dreams or fears. A rapidly repeated series of knocks awakened me. Someone was at the door. I checked my watch. It was two o'clock in the morning. "It's me," a man's voice was calling urgently, yet softly.

"Who?" I demanded, not recognizing the voice as that of Miguelito or any of the European adventurers from my tour group.

"The cabdriver," came a whispered reply. "Open the door. I must talk to you."

I hesitated, then rose from my bed and cracked the door open. I looked out, and recognized the taxi driver who had taken me to Miguelito's house.

Standing with his back to the moonlit sea, he demanded dollars. For Cubans other than the highest government officials, possession of foreign currency was a crime so serious that I figured he must be either an ordinary corrupt bureaucrat taking a chance or someone with genuine power, a Party member or police informer.

I paid him, saying "Yes, of course, I understand." I held up one hand to indicate there was no need to explain.

He left, smiling graciously, and I went back to bed consumed by a sudden rush of fear for Miguelito's safety. When I went to my cousin's house planning to tell him he was not forgotten, I had no idea that he would turn out to be a self-described quiet dissident, someone particularly vulnerable to being denounced by informers or neighborhood spies. Miguelito was already devastated by his father's suicide and his own anguish.

I stayed awake the rest of the night, thinking of my cousin singing inside his crater of discouragement. With his broken guitar he had chanted the words of his father's last song, the song Miguel wrote just before hanging himself.

The song was a wistful *guajiro* melody praising the hot green land of Miguel's youth. The lyrics painted a landscape of hills, cane fields and winding trails, caves, the sea, a sky filled with wild horses. And something about flying.

I could think of nothing but Miguel's death and Miguelito's despair. He'd seen the withering of his father's hope, the silencing of a man who had once inspired whole armies of rebel patriots with songs of liberation. Miguelito, I realized, had not been the only one with "nothing left to lose." Perhaps those words were first spoken by his father.

The next morning, I got up early and again evaded my guides, telling them I was going into Havana on a shopping spree. As long as they thought I was putting money into the treasure chests of the Maximum Leader, they seemed satisfied that my solitary journeys were just expressions of the independence of *Yanquis* . North Americans were now as welcome as any other tourists as long as they brought dollars into Cuba. In fact, the guides knew that tourism in Cuba was prohibited by the U.S. government. As part of the economic embargo, U.S. citizens were not supposed to spend money in Cuba. If we did, and if we were caught after returning to the U.S., the penalties were potentially very high–fines and prison terms. The *Cubatur* guides must have perceived me as someone willing to break my own country's laws, at great risk, in exchange for a little tropical leisure. In my case it wasn't true because I had obtained a U.S. Treasury Department permit, and I only wanted to dig up my past and offer a few words of encouragement.

In the morning sun, standing under a cascade of yellow cassia flowers, I wondered whether the taxi driver had kept his mouth shut about my visit to the private home of a Cuban family. If he'd revealed my secret, the guides might have been unwilling to let me get away from them again. I could be deported.

After many attempts to make me participate in organized activities, the guide who had tried to make my phone calls for me had finally given up, explaining to me that if she were blamed for my disobedience, there could be serious problems for her, not for me. She, after all, was Cuban.

In the hotel cafeteria I quickly drank three demitasses of strong Cuban coffee, and ate a plate of cheese with candied guava paste. Then I went out on the highway alone, deciding to take the *guagua* instead of a Tourist-Taxi.

I hoped that if I kept my camera hidden and addressed strangers as comrade, I might be able to blend into the crowds roaming Old Havana's melancholy streets.

The bus ride was just as hot and crowded as the rides I remembered taking on *guaguas* when I was in Havana as a child. In 1960, the *guagua* was a raucous, exuberant source of misery and discomfort, brimming with dozens of rapid musical conversations. Now the bus, like nearly everything else in Cuba, was brooding and silent.

I got off at a tree-lined *plaza* and sat on a park bench, looking around at the people and statues, wondering whether prayer was the only means I had to try to help my tormented cousin. I had taken an instant liking to Miguelito and Aurora, and felt certain that if my husband and I had lived in Cuba, or if my cousin and his wife somehow escaped and moved to the U.S., we might all become close companions. Miguelito had treated me with trust and sincerity. His inquisitiveness had been a welcome change from the materialistic conversations of tourists I'd encountered at the beach and in the hotel. I was tired of listening to their complaints about the lack of toilet seats in Cuba, the coarse texture of the toilet paper, the poor quality of the restaurant food, the inefficiency of communist salespeople in dollar shops.

When they came to me with their complaints about errors on hotel bills or the obstinacy of their guides, I wanted to shout, "Listen, my cousin is thinking of hanging himself and all you care about is toilet seats!"

I sat on the park bench, dwelling on thoughts of suicide, angels, demons. First there had been the Indians. Of the myriad Cuban Indians Columbus encountered on the island, how many had killed themselves? Five or ten thousand, fifty thousand, one hundred thousand? When the Conquistadors tried to enslave them for the purpose of mining Cuba's sparse traces of gold from mountain streams, the Taínos, Siboney and Guanahacabibe ate bitter manioc without first extracting the poison. They smothered their babies, strangled the older children, hanged themselves from trees. Spanish priests described entire forests weighed down by the corpses dangling from branches, the bodies of those who chose suicide over slavery.

Suicide is contagious. Amparo once told me about a time when it passed through our family like a virus, claiming so many men that the women wore mourning for twenty years. First an uncle killed himself, then his brother followed. Soon a son of the first man who committed suicide, then another brother. The women wore nothing but black and white for two decades, five years for each life, a small penance for such devastation, my grandmother said.

In my family, when a man commits suicide, no one tells his mother.

The old woman lives out the rest of her life believing her grown son died mysteriously before his time. My grandmother in New York didn't know that her brother Miguel had died by his own hand. After Miguelito took me into the cursed room, Aurora warned me not to say anything in front of the widow. Even Miguel's wife did not know the truth about his death. She was considered too weak to stand the shock.

My Cuban relatives believe in hiding sorrow from old people, especially old women. Year after year, decade after decade, everyone conspires to bury any terrible secret. I figured Miguelito would not have told me about his father's suicide unless he perceived me as strong enough to survive the news. I assumed Miguel must have assessed his son's strengths in the same manner before he decided to warn him of his own impending death.

But I didn't know whether the chosen confidante was expected to help deter the final act of defiance, and I certainly didn't know how to help.

I rose from the park bench. By now the tropical sun was fiery, gleaming metal in a clear blue sky. In Cuba, rain rarely falls in the morning, even during the height of the rainy season. At dawn the sky is clear, and by mid-afternoon it is raging black, a herd of turbulent clouds ready to stampede.

It was still early but I got in line to buy ice cream, the only abundant food on the island that year and one of the few which could be obtained on the streets by a foreigner with no ration coupons. I wasn't hungry, but there was an infectious hunting instinct in Havana's atmosphere, and the sight of people lining up for a generous serving of the rich, sweet cream awakened in me a primitive urge to join them.

The line was still short. I only had to wait half an hour before it was my turn for a three-scoop serving. A blackboard listed the flavors available that day, in this case vanilla.

I noticed that many people spent long moments pretending to study the menu even though it only listed vanilla. The revolution was not without its humor. I ate all three scoops, feeling cheerful yet perplexed by all the contradictions around me, the abundance of beer and ice cream in spite of the scarcity of nutritious food staples, the quiet drunks on street corners, men who, in other countries, might have felt free to be loud and obnoxious without fear of reprisals.

Cubans still knew how to make light of their misery. Miguelito had told me that the government had just invented a hamburger imitation to appease the Cuban appetite for variety, to give Cubans the illusion of abundance. The hamburgers were jokingly referred to on the street as

"McCastro burgers". Miguelito had also said, lightheartedly, that perhaps Fidel believed the Cuban people should be grateful to him for guarding their cholesterol levels by making sure that meat was hardly ever available.

I recalled a joke I'd heard among Cuban exiles in the U.S., about a teacher asking a student to compare the economy before and after the revolution. "Before," the child answered, "the economy was teetering on the brink of a precipice and after, it took a step forward."

I returned to the Central Plaza to get my bearings and looking up, noticed, once again, the army of marble angels perched on the facade of an old colonial building.

Seeing the statues of angels, I was reminded that even if I couldn't think of any other way to help my cousin, at least I could pray that the demons swarming across Miguel's house would be defeated. Facing evil, I decided, was the swiftest path to becoming aware of good.

I decided to find Miguelito's house again right away, walking to avoid the taxi drivers who might keep demanding bribes.

Making my way along the quiet streets, I was struck by the similarities between Havana and Harlem. People lingered on the streets even though the streets were dangerous. In Harlem they risked being mugged or knifed. In Havana they simply risked being overheard. In both cities everyone was constantly wary, alert to the point of exhaustion. In both the atmosphere was one of predation, as in a primitive hunting society where people circled around one another, afraid of cannibals, but needing to be out, searching, prowling.

In Havana, at least the buildings were still elegant, ornamented with their crumbling medieval gargoyles and chiseled marble angels. In Old Havana the mail slots were strange scowling faces carved into colonial stone walls, their mouths open to receive letters.

Submerged beneath the deep layer of communal melancholy, I walked carrying the burden of my cousin's pain, remembering the stories Gabriel had told me about storms so violent they ripped winged statues from their pedestals and sent them flying. At the time it had seemed like a fantasy, but later I read about such storms in Cuban history books.

I ambled along the stone sea wall; scattered groups of boys and young men sat on the wall, looking out, away from the island. Others walked silently, gazing toward El Morro Castle.

The voice of a solitary man reached me. "Here by the sea," he sang softly, "on the dead-end street of my memory..."

I walked away from his song, through a group of men whispering as they discussed an impending attack by the U.S. Navy. "We are surrounded..." I had heard it often since arriving in Cuba. Nearly everyone seemed to believe the stories told on Cuban State television news programs, about *Yanqui* forces constantly preparing to attack Cuba. The threat kept people anxious, and it aroused the fierce nationalism so many Cubans felt whenever a bigger country tried to swallow the island.

A tour group from Spain was following an official guide along the sea wall. "Cuba," the guide's voice came floating along with the sea breeze, "is paradise." It was the only loud and confident voice I'd heard all day.

On the morning of Gabriel's arrest he sat very still, his chest pressed forward against the wavy mane of his horse. One war leads to the next, he thought, remembering all the wars of his mother's lifetime.

He watched his sons in the distance, carrying the big metal milk cans. Again, the milk would have to stay on the farm and be made into cheese. The roads would not be safe. In town, Amparo and Isabelita would be worried. They would wonder why he never brought fresh milk to Trinidad anymore. The distance was not great. During good times he rode into town every day with milk and fruit for his sisters and his aging mother. At least he could depend on Amparo and Isabelita to refrain from talking about the trouble around their mother. She was too old for such sadness and, anyway, what could she do to help? The rumors would only make her worry at first and then she would start praying, keeping her worry secret from everybody except God. Weren't there already enough secrets floating around?

Daniel had said the islanders were all secretive because they descended from Columbus' men, Andalusians who kept their mouths sealed with seven locks and seven keys. No one could keep a secret as well as a Cuban, Daniel had said. Even the women, when they gossiped, never told their truly deep secrets. And of all women, Amparo could always be trusted to wait for God's will. When she was very young she'd talked of becoming a nun, but later she met a man who danced so well that all she'd wanted out of life was to marry him and spend her days dancing. Their mother had disapproved, saying that men who danced that well could become dangerous. Amparo wouldn't marry without her mother's approval, so she gave up her first true love and later married a stern, serious churchgoing man given to inexplicable rages, a man who died young, consumed by his own fury.

Meanwhile, Miguel was himself becoming one of the best dancers on the island, and a singer and songwriter as well. It made their mother sad to think of all her children leaving the farm, but as long as Gabriel was there, she felt that they were all safe in the world, with a few caballerías of good sugar land to shelter them whenever the outside world went crazy.

When Amparo's only daughter wandered even further than Havana, marrying a stranger and leaving the island entirely, everyone had assumed she'd come back often to visit. But the years had turned into a time of revolution, and now here was another war looming, just when they'd all thought the freedom they'd been fighting for had finally arrived.

Gabriel couldn't help smiling when he remembered how overjoyed his mother had been on the day Fidel's ragged Barbudos marched into Havana. Machado and Batista had let the Yanquis take over too much farmland, nearly half of all the sugar land on the island. Cuba's guajiros were all jubilant when Fidel Castro won, thinking now finally their precious bits of land would be safe from the rich foreign sugar mills which were always trying to take it away from the poor independent farmers by buying them out when prices went bad and times were hard.

How excited they'd been, all of them, even Daniel who knew history and hardly ever trusted any leader. Even Daniel who'd fought against Machado during the 1930's. They'd all hated Machado with a passion. The tyrant had sold off Cuba's forests of mahogany, ebony and cedar to foreigners who wanted the wood for furniture, church pews, even railroad ties. Machado's secret police were the worst bullies anyone could remember, worse than the Spanish soldiers during the wars for independence. While Machado was in power, ordinary people disappeared just for singing songs considered defiant. Imagine, Gabriel had said to his brothers, how could a song be considered dangerous? And next thing he knew, Daniel was out in the streets of Havana, fighting, and Miguel was right beside him, singing.

Machado, it was said, had been so corrupt he took the people's money and used it to buy an enormous diamond for himself, which he inlaid into the floor of a palace. Later, Batista ended up being very much like Machado, siphoning off the people's wealth and injecting the venom of secret police, just as Machado had, to inspire a fear of speaking out.

Machado's police had chased Daniel all the way to the farm, where he hid under the big ceiba while they threatened the family, demanding information on his whereabouts. That was the day Gabriel truly learned to appreciate his mother's courage. He'd watched, astounded, as his mother lied to the police, calmly insisting, over and over, that no, she had no idea where her son could be, didn't they know he was a student in Havana, why didn't they go back to the city and look for him there, at the University.

At night she sneaked past the police and took food to Daniel while he waited under the vast drooping branches of the ceiba tree, a drizzle of kapok coating him with silky fiber. The fugitive made a bed for himself out of leaves and kapok, and with the food his mother brought him, he was able to stay under the ceiba tree for days, waiting for the police to give up and go away. When they finally left, disgusted with the stubborn resilience of peasants, Daniel came out laughing, saying no wonder run-away African slaves had believed ceiba trees could get up and dance at night, no wonder they held the trees sacred and dug holes in the red soil to feed the roots with offerings of wild mountain herbs, garlic and rum.

"The walls recede, the roof vanishes, and you float quite naturally, you float uprooted, dragged off, lifted high..." Words from a Reinaldo Arenas poem haunted me as I walked along the sea wall known as *El Malecón*, gazing across the harbor at the medieval stone walls of El Morro Castle, where for so many centuries, under so many rulers, Cubans, including Arenas and many other poets, had been tortured in dungeons, not for their crimes, but for their words.

Finally I turned away from the sea, and plunged back into the network of narrow streets, making my way toward Miguelito's house, contemplating the futility of torturing poets for their words. Of all the things that inspire people to write poetry, prison walls have always been the most effective. Poets always find ways to smuggle out their words, scribbled on toilet paper

or on remnants of torn shirt sleeves or bedsheets. Cuban poets had perfect-
ed the world's tiniest writing. Of all the ways to silence people, arresting
them, I thought, was the least logical. In prison, people write on the walls.
They memorize entire books. They devise codes. The very thing it most
feared was the thing each tyranny promoted.

I arrived at my cousin's house anxious to give his wife the food I'd
saved from last night's hotel buffet. I decided I would not tell Miguelito
about my experiences witnessing the suicide attempt of a *totí* bird and
being bribed by a cabdriver.

Miguelito answered the door just as he had before, after a long delay. I
realized he must have spent some time looking out the window to see who
was knocking. Perhaps if it had been a spy from the Neighborhood Committee, he would have needed to hide a few things, papers, books, the guitar with its broken strings. As a dissident, he would be watched constantly.
Even now, some neighbor was probably noting and recording the arrival of
a stranger.

My cousin welcomed me just as he had the day before, warmly, as if I
had been visiting him every day of his life. Today he seemed less agitated,
more contemplative. We moved about the house, chatting with his mother
and wife. He helped his wife tend to their child's demands, and they discussed ordinary household topics—food, laundry, the cat.

Aurora seemed terribly anxious today. When we were alone in the
kitchen, she said, once more, "What will become of us?" I assumed it was
something she said often to everyone. I had no answer. There was no way
to assure her that Cuba would be like East Germany, with a wall of Communism ready to crumble overnight. I couldn't tell her that the U.S. would
step in and rescue her besieged island. There were no signs of immediate
change, only the ever-deepening silence, the lengthening ration lines, and
the dwindling fuel supplies. Only a few symbolic reforms had been granted
by the Maximum Leader in an effort to conjure the illusion of freedom.
The right to own a Bible, for instance, or to sing in churches which, a few
years earlier, had been banned. Miguelito said he wouldn't go to church
because certainly many of the newly recruited clergy members would turn
out to be police informers. "Imagine going to confession!" he shuddered.

"Once," Aurora confided, whispering to avoid hurting her mother-in-
law's feelings, "we had a Bible in the house, a long time ago, but the old
lady was afraid they might decide to search the house, so she made us get
rid of it, just to be safe. And to think, now suddenly these things are

allowed, no longer called "the opiate of the people." She smiled, and I sensed that she had never been afraid to get caught owning a Bible. Her dread came from something else, something I couldn't identify. She spoke openly of being a dissident, even though she repeated several times her fear of speaking honestly to her own sister who, she repeated often, was "*muy comunista*," very communist.

"We're very careful to whom we talk," she assured me. "We select our friends." She told me how Daniel used to come to the house to visit Miguel, and how the two brothers would sit in that music-filled room complaining bitterly about Fidel's government. I tried to imagine the day when they first realized that they'd supported a man who had ended up demanding that he be referred to as Maximum Leader. I pictured the two of them in the days when they were younger and still hopeful, debating the final outcome of the revolution that had promised freedom and justice. Would it have been after Fidel forced a newly elected President out of power and replaced him with a puppet government? Or perhaps when it became clear that hundreds of Cubans were being sent to the firing squads of El Morro Castle without first standing trial. The change of heart could have begun with Fidel's dissolution of institutions, the labor unions, agricultural and professional associations, the political parties. Or perhaps the monstrous revelation came only after Gabriel was arrested.

I followed Aurora around the house, from kitchen to bedroom, chatting about the dwindling food supply and the makeshift alcohol-burning stove Miguelito had improvised so his wife could keep cooking near the end of each month, when the fuel rations ran out The refrigerator was empty. A handful of precious yams and *malanga* tubers sat on the counter, displayed like gemstones. Aurora complained that her son needed clothes. He'd outgrown his shoes and wouldn't receive new ones until the end of the year. She lamented the visits of snooping neighbors. "They come over all the time," she moaned, "poking into every room, noticing what kind of pictures we hang on the walls, which music is being played on the radio, which magazines are lying around next to the toilet."

By now it was clear to me that Maximum Leader had consolidated his power not just by military force or political manipulations, but by ravaging the traditional Latin American family and community support systems, by creating a nightmarish existence where people were terrified of their own siblings and neighbors as well as strangers.

Miguelito joined us, helping with the housework and talking excitedly about the Neighborhood Committees. "When it's my turn to spy on the neighbors," he told me, "I don't show up. When I'm expected to attend some meeting or rally, I don't go!" My cousin seemed so full of defiance he looked like he might burst.

"You've heard the joke about the Cuban dog?" Miguelito asked. I shook my head. "Well," my cousin began. "You see, there was this communist dog who ate well and had everything he needed because he belonged to a military family, so he was a very privileged dog. But one day he climbed into a fishing boat and set sail for Miami. When his boat landed on the beach in Florida, a lot of American dogs gathered around him and asked, 'Why did you leave Cuba if you lacked neither food nor shelter?' And the dog replied, 'I was just dying to bark.'

"In Cuba," Miguelito explained, "so many little things are prohibited that a person couldn't possibly remember them all. The list of things which are prohibited is much longer than the list of things you're allowed to do."

My cousin and his wife began asking questions about the outside world. They wanted to know everything, every detail.

"Is it true," Miguelito asked, "that in your country you are allowed to vote for a new president when you get tired of the old one?"

"After four years," I answered, "the president can be re-elected or replaced. After eight years he's out, no matter what."

My cousin and his wife gazed at each other, stunned. "You see," Miguelito said to his wife, quietly. "It's true. We listen to Radio Martí," he explained, turning back to me. We had all migrated toward a big ornately carved dining room table surrounded by ebony-inlaid chairs. "Here we get only government news, so I hide a short-wave radio and every night we listen to news from Miami. We hear these things, but since our news is so full of lies we never know what to believe, so we hear these things from over there and we're not sure whether they could actually be true."

He sat silent for a moment, contemplating my answer, I imagined, or choosing his next question. "Tell me," he finally said, "is it true that over there anyone can walk into a store and buy a gun? Do people really keep weapons in their houses?"

I nodded yes.

"And what about drugs, how many people do you know, you yourself personally, who have taken dangerous drugs? Here they tell us that you over there have great weaknesses and terrible problems."

"Too many to count," I replied, thinking of opium and dragons, satyrs, fauns, sea nymphs...sorcerers...utopias.

"And how many people do you know, you personally, who have died of AIDS? Here, of course, everyone has been tested, and all who are infected have been sent away to...well, to leper colonies, you might say."

I said I knew several who'd died of AIDS, of gang wars, of giving up. I said New York, like Havana, had its underworld of despair.

Miguelito looked at Aurora, and she returned his quizzical glance. They seemed like they were trying to appraise my answers, find meaning in the similarities and contrasts between our two separated orbits around the same world. They were realizing, I imagined, that the U.S. is not, after all, paradise.

"Every place has its problems," I said and both nodded to agree.

I thought of all the years I'd spent in Spanish Harlem, firmly believing that Cuba was paradise. I knew my family had supported the revolution. I knew Alvaro and many of my other distant cousins had fought alongside Fidel Castro and Che Guevara in the wild mountains of eastern and central Cuba. I knew some of my *Barbudo* cousins had died fighting for freedom from Batista's tyranny. I knew Gabriel had given food to the rebels, proud to be helping men who were bearing all the promises of the island's noble and passionate coat-of-arms.

Until my own relatives began to arrive with the refugees, I assumed that my cousins couldn't possibly have died for anything less than that which had been promised.

"Most of my life," I told Miguelito, "I thought that if only we had stayed in Cuba I would have been happy. Much of my life," I continued, despite my cousin's expression of disbelief, "I thought of Cuba as the only place where people were actually free."

The freedom I remembered was a different face of freedom than the one Miguelito imagined. I had spent my years in Harlem yearning for Gabriel's wilderness, for the breakneck rides on his barely tamed horses, the descendants of animals his father caught wild in the mountains. To me, free had meant feral.

"Here," Miguelito said after a thoughtful pause, leaning forward across the worn mahogany table, "they always tell us the bad things about your country. What interests me," he continued, "is that you yourself are aware of some of those bad things too. Here, when something bad happens, when someone is murdered or robbed, they keep it secret. You won't read about it in the newspaper. Here, everything is pretense, illusion. We are ruled by a magician."

"Aah," I sighed, suddenly wondering about my uncle Juan back in New York. When he'd arrived as a refugee from Cuba, he'd refused to read any written words at all, even the newspapers. He didn't allow magazines in his house, insisting that they were all full of lies and couldn't be trusted. At the time I'd simply viewed him as an eccentric relative, but now I understood that perhaps he'd simply grown sick of hypocrisy.

I realized how little I really knew about uncle Juan, my mother's brother, and about all the other relatives who fled the island. Even Amparo, my grandmother, had told me about ration lines and how hard it was to wait for hours never knowing whether they'd run out before your turn came and send you away empty-handed. She'd told me about short-ages of the most basic items, even sacks for carrying your food away from the ration outlets. Once, when she didn't have a single bottle or container of any sort, she'd taken a porcelain vase with her to wait in line for her rationed cooking oil. The vase had been given to her as a gift by the danc-ing man before her mother chased him away, forbidding their marriage. It was a white vase covered with delicate painted flowers, a vase made in Spain and brought to Cuba centuries earlier by some predecessor of the mysterious dancing man my grandma still loved, even though she married someone else, and loved him too, and had her children and her grandchil-dren, and even though she never knew what became of the dancing man, who went away to Havana and was never heard from again. I remembered how Amparo's eyes grew distant when she told me how they filled her vase with cooking oil, and how some of the other women in line were envious because they hadn't been able to find any kind of container at all, and had to leave the line with just two handfuls of cooking oil carried in their cupped palms, and most of it spilled before they could carry it home, and when they arrived, they found that all they had was enough oil to coat their skin as protection from the sun. Amparo told me she'd carried ground meat home that way, cupped in her hands to keep it from falling onto the street, because she couldn't find any sort of box or bag to put it in. Half-starved dogs had followed her home, threatening her with their snarls, leering at the meat. My grandma said she was sure the dogs would tear her hands off along with the meat, and when she made it home safely, her hands still intact, the bits of meat still clinging to them, she thanked God for His mercy, she told Him that if He would just do one more thing for her before she died, she hoped it would be sending her out of Cuba because she didn't want to spy on her neighbors.

"They asked me to head up the neighborhood Committee for the Defense of the Revolution," my *Abuelita* had explained to me when I'd asked her why she wanted to leave the place that was supposed to be paradise.

"But I didn't want to spy on the neighbors," was my grandma's answer, "What a horror!" She'd rolled her eyes to show me how impolite spying was. She had been raised properly by her peasant mother, and even though they never had much education or money, *guajiros* were people, she insisted, who knew right from wrong. "So I said, thank you so much, I'm very flattered, of course, to be selected for such an honor, but I'm getting old and my health is failing, my eyesight especially, so really I couldn't do justice to such a great and important responsibility. You must forgive me if I decline."

"And then," *Abuelita* had continued, sitting comfortably in her New York kitchen, gazing out her window at a landscape of snow and concrete, "and then I applied for permission to emigrate, and I was persecuted for wanting to leave, they called me worm and parasite and pig, and I lost all privileges; I had to take whatever was left over in the ration lines. Once you admit that you want to leave they treat you like a criminal. I was lucky they didn't send me to the work camps."

For Juan it had been the same, a maze of deception. He left the island several years before his mother Amparo did. He had been preparing for the Olympics. His picture had been taken with Fidel Castro himself, and the other Olympic hopefuls of his team. Juan was a tremendous success, an Olympic athlete even though he was over thirty and his son Juanito was nearly fourteen. A success until they asked him to join the Communist Party. It was supposed to be Cuba's greatest honor. Juan declined, saying "thank you, I am very flattered, but my wife has left Cuba, and I have my son of course, so as you can see, I have family problems. I must go to Miami and try to bring her back, and then we'll see." Juan's wife had not left yet, but after he turned down Party membership she got away immediately, taking Juanito who was almost old enough to be drafted and sent to Central America or Angola. Soon after, Juan followed, sacrificing his Olympic career and leaving behind everything, all his trophies and his papers, even the photograph of his team with Fidel Castro Ruz, *Presidente de la República*, signed in one corner by *El Líder Máximo*.

Amparo assured me that she'd hidden all of Tío Juan's things in a safe place, along with her own family photographs, because she was allowed to take nothing when she left Cuba, not even photographs, not even her wedding ring or rosary. She left with just the dress she was wearing and her memories.

Suddenly I realized that Miguelito and Aurora had been waiting patiently during my long moment of silent reminiscence. I smiled, embarassed. "I was just thinking how full of surprises life is," I explained, still thinking of uncle Juan and his distrust of periodicals, a distrust I now understood.

"How many different kinds of magazines and newspapers do you have over there?" Aurora asked.

"Thousands," I guessed. Perhaps tens of thousands, I didn't really know.

My cousin's wife was astonished. "No! Thousands? Really?"

I nodded. Aurora's eyes were wide. She laughed. The thought of thousands of different printed opinions made her dizzy with delight. "What a marvel," she said, wandering off toward the kitchen, calling back, "Here we have only the government publications. Even those from the Soviet Union have been banned because they talk about nothing but *perestroika* and *glasnost* these days."

"I bought the radio by selling my mother's jewelry," Miguelito said, leaning back in one of the inlaid chairs, his hand resting on the mane of a lion carved into the wood. "If you sell valuables to the government they let you into the dollar stores to buy things you can't get otherwise. That's how desperate for money this government is. But it is also very corrupt. In this government there are some very rich people, millionaires, incredibly rich. Someday the horror stories will come out. Someday the people will seek revenge. It will be just like Romania, you'll see.

"I would like to see a plebiscite," my cousin continued calmly. The angry despair of the previous day had been softened. "Why not? In every country they are having elections. We are the last."

It was true. Cuba and China were two of the last nations where Communism still lingered.

"If you write about me," my cousin said, peering at me with a hopeful gleam in his eyes, "don't use my real name."

"Write about you?" I asked, stunned. Amparo must have written to Miguel before his death. She must have told him about my poetry.

"Oh no," I laughed, "you've misunderstood. I don't write that kind of thing. I'm just a nature poet. I write very small, insignificant little things about trees and flowers, birds, insects, things like that." I thought about my life at home with my husband and children in the North, in the quiet outskirts of a rural town that looked like it belonged in a cowboy movie.

I had been living there quite oblivious to the outside world, when suddenly memories of Cuba started floating back, especially memories of Gabriel, who had been arrested, and of his verdant farm which, according to Amparo and Juan, no longer existed. When the memories started drifting back into my life, I volunteered to write letters on behalf of political prisoners, and I began applying for permission to visit relatives in Cuba. And as the human rights bulletins began arriving, I realized, by reading them, that among the names, I would occasionally find a distant cousin.

Now, as I sat with one of these cousins at the beautiful table he'd inherited from Cuba's devastated forests, I listened as Miguelito explained that he would like me to write about his life for him, because he lived in a place of terror where such an act would be too dangerous for his family. If he were caught writing about the silence and hypocrisy, he would be labeled dangerous. Even his identity card would carry the words, arrested for *peligrosidad*, for dangerousness. His wife would probably lose her job. His son would not be allowed to study the professions. Aptitude and studiousness were not the criteria used to select students for desirable programs. The child was judged by his parents' dedication to Communism. If my cousin found himself designated as someone "in a dangerous state of mind", then his whole family might be sent out to work in the fields, confined to forced labor camps.

My cousin wanted to be heard. I couldn't sing for him, not the way he would sing, but at least I could write a naïve and simplified version of his words. I could memorize them and later, in the safety of the North, surrounded by irrigated fruit trees and howling coyotes, I could write them down and hope that people in the outside world might imagine Miguelito's songs.

Since arriving on the island I'd noticed that Cubans often waved at tour buses. They blew kisses to the tourists, even though they should have been bitter about wealthy foreigners eating the people's food, treasured food which should have been parceled out to the ration lines. Suddenly I understood that many were happy to see us, the outsiders, maybe because they wanted us to go home and take their stories with us. They were hoping we would tell our friends what we had seen in Cuba, nearly eleven million people being strangled.

Miguelito was still watching me, waiting for my answer. "I won't use my own real name either," I assured my cousin.

—⌒∽—

On the morning of his arrest, Gabriel felt a vibrant sun heating the skin of his machete-hardened fist. He gripped the reins, kicked his stallion and cantered toward the house, where his wife was ringing a cow bell to announce breakfast. Gabriel waved at her, noticing the fullness of her aging body, and the way grandchildren trailed behind her gathered skirt, following her like chicks behind a hen. To Gabriel, the sound of her cow bell was both mournful and welcoming, like the sound of a conch-shell trumpet, a century earlier, on one of the big plantations, calling the slaves in to dinner.

Today he would tell her what he'd heard from Alvaro. He would tell her the rumors from town about troops being stationed on all the big farms to keep the new Alzado rebels from coming down from the mountains in search of food and other supplies. They would need medicines, boots, ammunition. If it turned out like before, no one would refuse to help. No guajiro would refuse to feed boys who were fighting against a new tyrant, especially if the new one planned to start seizing ordinary farms, small farms along with the foreign-owned sugar giants.

Gabriel cantered toward his bohío remembering his wife the way she looked when he first met her, the great-granddaughter of Basque shepherds, a woman accustomed to living on harsh land, a good strong country girl who didn't waste time longing for plumbing or electricity. For her, their outdoor shower stall with its bucket of cold water was more than enough luxury. Someday Gabriel planned to build her a stone house with a stone floor. In that floor he planned to inlay many small cross-sections of the stalactites from the caves by the sea where once the timid Siboney had lived peacefully, with nothing to fear but the hurricanes, sharks, and raids by cannibals in their big canoes. Those caves had served the cimarrón African slaves well, long after the last Indians had been slaughtered. The caverns were big, yellow glowing chambers filled with mysterious underground streams, even waterfalls, and inexplicable specks of light which somehow reached into the depths from tiny hidden openings above, openings revealing intensely blue sky and explosive black clouds. Underground, practically the entire island was connected by caves.

Once there had been so many bats in the caves that guajiros made a regular business out of harvesting the guano and selling it to the foreigners as fertilizer for their big sugar fields.

Gabriel rode toward his house still thinking about his wife and the rumors and the caves which could someday help him build a glowing golden floor for his imaginary stone house. You couldn't tell how beautiful the stalactites were until you got them out of the caves, where they could find the sunlight and really begin to radiate, like underground stars brought up into the sky. There were no dangerous animals in the caves, only a few majá boas too small to hurt a person. Escaped slaves had believed that one of those small boa constrictors could kill you with its poisonous breath, like the fiery breath of a dragon. The cimarrones said that after a thousand years each boa would turn into a sea serpent and swim out of the caves and into the ocean to swallow Spanish ships, the ships which brought slaves across the immeasurable sea from their African homes.

The slaves believed certain trees could get up at night and dance. They believed people could fly away from slavery, just get up out of the fields and barracoons and enter the sky, flying back to Nigeria or the Congo. When Gabriel was young there were still many men and women who had been born slaves and had only been free since the last days of Spanish rule. These people had sworn to Gabriel and the other children that at one time so many slaves flew away that entire plantations were crippled and had to close down their sugar mills because no one was left to load them with the heavy burdens of raw cane.

One of Gabriel's uncles married the daughter of a Congolese woman who had only been freed a few years before giving birth to the girl who would later become the wife of a guajiro. When Gabriel was a child, he thought his light uncle and dark aunt were the two happiest people he'd ever met. They acted like people who had found a way to trick the devil, laughing all the time, and singing, ignoring the pale town children who threw rocks at them when they rode into Trinidad on Sundays and feast days.

They had been the ones who took Gabriel and his brothers into the mountains and showed them the ruins of cimarrón villages buried deep in the shadowy, enigmatic forest. When Daniel saw the remains of false trails, and the deep pits covered over with leaves and armed with erect, sharpened bamboo stakes, he decided he would someday move away to Havana and study history and find out how the slaves figured out such ingenious ways of hiding and protecting their secret villages.

Years later, Daniel actually did it. He went away and became a historian and came back talking about rebellions and survival. He went up into the mountains and tried to live like a cimarrón, hunting wild pigs and harvesting wild honey and roots and tubers. He invited Gabriel up to his hideout to see how the cimarrones buried their gold in secret places, gold they obtained by trading food and wild honey to pirates who landed on the secluded beaches near Trinidad, rich but hungry. That was in the days when every treasure fleet had to pass through Cuba on its way from Mexico and South America to Imperial Spain, delivering the wealth of conquered Aztecs and Incas into the royal treasuries.

When Daniel told him about the cimarrón gold, Gabriel had thought it strange that escaped slaves who could never live out in the open would treasure a mineral which could only be spent in town. What good would it do them? Wasn't the wild honey itself more precious to a forest dweller than any amount of gold?

And Daniel had explained that the runaways always guarded a secret reservoir of hope. They had to hide in the forest in total silence, never singing or whistling, in case bounty hunters might be roaming the forests with their muskets and trained dogs, searching for escaped slaves to sell back to the planters.

"If a cimarrón traveled through the forest at night and saw a light," Daniel said, "then he might think it was a witch, and he would spread wild mustard seeds in his path as he walked, to paralyze the witches, because the cimarrones believed that once a witch stepped on a mustard seed, her feet would freeze to the spot and she could never move again.

"Runaways even had to be afraid of birds. In the forest there is a bird which whistles exactly like a man. A cimarrón could never be sure whether he was hearing the song of a bird or the whistle of a bounty hunter calling his dogs.

"Cimarrones were also afraid of the tocororo, that pretty bird with a stripe across its chest. The Spaniards said tocororos looked like they were wearing the uniform of the King of Spain, green with a scarlet sash. Any slave caught looking at a tocororo could be accused of disrespect, and would be whipped or sent to the stocks. Even after they were free and in hiding, the runaways kept on dreading these birds, with their short monotonous song, co, co, co, co.

"The cimarrones were afraid of sleep. They believed majá boas could suck out all your blood while you were sleeping. They believed the soul could wander away from a sleeping body and, if the body was awakened before the soul returned, a terrible sickness would result. But they said the sickness only affected the body, which stayed in the forest dying of fright, while the soul roamed free."

Gabriel approached the house, deciding that he would not tell his wife how sleepless he had been lately. He would not tell her he had been getting up at night, wandering around the farm, chasing the devil and shaking his fist. He would not tell her that he had developed a fear of sleep which overwhelmed him every night, when he lay awake thinking about the rumors, about Alvaro with his reptile-green uniform, and Alvaro's brothers Omar, Emilio and Adán, trekking up into the mountains, becoming Alzados–rebels–like so many guerrilla warriors before them, like Alvaro himself when he fought with Castro. Gabriel had been terrified of sleep, thinking that maybe the troops would come at night, and maybe among them he would find relatives and what would God think, brother fighting brother again, so soon, when a war had just ended. Worst of all, during those long dark hours when Gabriel's fear of sleep was profound and all-consuming, there was the gnawing rodent-like fear eating at Gabriel from the inside out, the fear that something might happen to his family and his farm.

Gabriel ate breakfast with his wife and sons and their wives and his daughters and their husbands and all his grandchildren, with the many people who all lived together under the single small thatched roof. Yes, one day they would need a bigger house, a stone house with a stone floor, a floor like gold, like cimarrón gold received from pirates in exchange for wild honey, gold you could bury and save as a reservoir of hope.

They ate, a fine meal of papaya with lime juice, and corn meal spiced with anise. They ate together in the open air, seated on stones and logs tossed about the farmyard like toys thrown by a giant. Gabriel sat on a four-legged Taíno stool, with its comfortable concave stone seat. Thousands of years old, Daniel had verified, when Gabriel found it intact under the protective branches of a ceiba tree in the mountains. A stool some chieftain sat on hundreds of years earlier, while eating a meal much like this one, shared with all his family.

Gabriel finished his breakfast rapidly, then set about telling his grandchildren stories about the Indians and escaped slaves. He told them how the runaways liked to raid their old plantations at Christmas, during the dry season when it was easy for them to race back into the mountains with looted weapons and food.

"But they didn't really make the raids to capture guns and meat. No, they went to free their enslaved families, and friends too. They went to the plantations looking for their parents and sisters and wives and cousins. They could have taken jewelry and silver from the big houses of the masters, but instead they carried off the other slaves, and set them free. But during the first three years no one captured in a raid was allowed to leave those secret villages hidden in the mountains.

"First each one had to prove his loyalty to the cause of freedom. Because even among slaves there would always be a few who couldn't stand the hard life of the wilderness and would try to go back to the plantation with information about the secret villages, and these ones were dangerous. Nothing is more dangerous than information when you are trying to hide."

Of all the grandchildren, the only one who always seemed captivated by Gabriel's repetitions of Daniel's tales was the boy Gabriel called Taíno, because he was timid and serious. His face had the mahogany skin and black eyes of an Indian.

"Tell me about the Lottery," Taíno demanded, and Gabriel took him onto his knee, and told him once again how in Cuba the servants came from many different countries, not just Africa but China also, and all the African slaves and indentured Chinese and all their Cuban-born offspring, all might be allowed, on certain plantations, to work overtime on Sundays instead of resting, in order to save up a little money of their own to try to buy themselves free.

"Only it took so long to earn enough to buy oneself free," Gabriel told the boy, "that by the time you were free you were also very old, too old to work. It was a trick of the masters, really, because by the time a slave was old enough to buy himself free, he would just be a burden anyway and, then, as a weak and useless old man, he could be set free to go off in search of his own place to live and his own food, and the master wouldn't have to take care of him while he waited for death.

"So the Lottery was the only way out. It was the same Imperial Lottery everyone else played, a game set up by the King of Spain. Slaves were allowed to buy tickets just like anyone else, only the tickets were expensive, so the slaves had to use their little bits of money from working overtime on Sunday, and they had to pool all their money together, and sometimes a group of slaves would win and there would be enough money to free them all. Imagine how they must have felt on that day, walking up to the master's house with their winnings, saying, very respectfully, 'Sir, we've come to buy ourselves free.'

"And for those who never won the Lottery, and could never hope to be free, unless they ran away or lived to be very old, well, there was always Kings' Day, that one day each year when slaves were allowed to make fun of their masters by dressing up like Spaniards and dancing. What a carnival that must have been, eh? Each group of slaves dressed like Ladies or Lords, priests even, and soldiers too.

"The slaves worked very hard to perfect their costumes for that celebration. And their dances. They invented many dances because during those days dancing was one of very few things the slaves were allowed to do. Practically everything else was forbidden, but dancing was permitted. Slaves invented the rumba, which imitates a rooster fluffing its feathers for the hen, who keeps pecking away in the barnyard, pretending not to notice, but really, of course, she's watching the rooster very closely out of the corner of her eye. And the conga, some say it looks like a line of slaves chained together in the form of a serpent, dancing.

"You know, even today, many people believe that if you dance well enough, and long enough, a spirit comes into you, and it could be a good spirit or a bad one, there's no way to tell, until it's too late, so you have to be very careful if you call out to the spirits. The slaves could dance until they turned into the spirit of the river, or the spirit of the ocean or the mountains or war or gold, even the spirit of disease, or the devil himself."

Then Gabriel went on to tell Taíno about the Indians for whom he was nicknamed. "They believed that since turtles are shaped like the womb, like the bellies of pregnant women, people must have descended from a turtle-woman, something your uncle Daniel calls the primordial turtle-mother. The Taínos knew about the great flood. Everyone on earth knew about it, because it was sent over the whole world, and very few escaped. The Taínos believed that only men survived the great flood. So, after the flood, the men went out and found a turtle-woman and married her. But they never trusted her completely because turtles are very dangerous when you're swimming. If a turtle jumps on your back while you're under water, it can drag you down to the bottom of the sea and it will never let you go. You drown."

Gabriel saw how his wife was looking at him, quizzical and fond, yet disapproving. "Such tales you tell the child," she said, shaking her head. One would think you had seen these things yourself. As if you've ever been to the bottom of the sea!"

"But that's not all," Gabriel continued, winking at his wife, who picked up his plate and walked with it toward the wash tub, calling out to one of the girls to bring her water from the well because all three of the big ceramic tinajón jars were almost empty.

"Unless it rains," Gabriel's wife called out behind her, "we'll have to fill them up all the way."

"It will rain," Gabriel assured her, interrupting his stories to glance up at the sky, where dark clouds were already beginning to mass. Gabriel liked to imagine that each of the clouds was a horse with its rider, transforming the sky into an entire army of valiant warriors.

"You know what the Taínos believed about guava trees, don't you?" Gabriel asked his grandson. All the other children had drifted away toward the pasture and barn, looking for more active forms of entertainment. He would have to remind them to start their chores or they would spend the morning tossing pebbles and chasing calves. "The Taínos said that ghosts roamed through the guava thickets at night. And do you know why they said this? Because the guava fruit, when it falls on the ground and rots, begins to smell like death. It is a smell you can detect from miles away and, no matter how much you love the taste of guava, no one has ever enjoyed that odor of fruit left rotting on the wet ground after a rain."

"That's enough, my love," called Gabriel's wife as she leaned over the washtub. "Don't tell him the part about ghosts looking for lovers. He's too young for that."

This time Gabriel's wink was directed at the boy, who rose and smiled at his grandfather, giving him a tilted-head expression that meant, 'Tell me.'

"Ah, well, yes, there is that too. The Taínos said that the ghosts in the guava thickets were not just looking for fruit to eat, but they were also waiting for humans to come along and be their lovers because that is what ghosts and demons do, wait for a chance to catch the living off guard."

"Hush, my love," Gabriel's wife ordered, turning to face him, her hair blowing up from her face which was growing red. Now he could see that she was truly angry.

"Oh, well," Gabriel winked at the boy, "I'll have to tell you the rest some other time."

"There's not much left," said his wife, scowling at him.

"Just the part about how you tell the dead from the living," said Gabriel, rising from the prehistoric stool. "I'm going down to the river now, Taíno. Come with me and we'll talk about more cheerful things, to make your grandma happy."

"Don't scare him with your tales," his wife called after them as they ambled away toward the river. "And don't let him fall in. The river is full, and he doesn't have braids for pulling him out."

Gabriel looked down at his little grandson and said, "She's right. The girls have long braids just so we can pull them out of the river if they fall in, but your hair is short, so you should start carrying your lariat everywhere you go, just in case. That way, if you fall in, especially now, when the river is still swollen from the last rains, you can rope a tree branch and pull yourself to shore."

Taíno, his face serious and serene, nodded. "Now tell me the rest, Abuelito," he demanded, "we're far enough so she can't hear us anymore."

"What, you expect me to betray your Abuelita's trust?"

The boy nodded.

"Oh well, a few months ago boys your age were up in the mountains fighting. Some may still be up there. Anyway, it's not so hard to tell the dead from the living. Ghosts don't have bellybuttons. Their middles are completely smooth. So if you have to go out into a guava thicket at night, although you won't do that, if you're smart, but if you ever do, stay away from women with no bellybuttons. The Indians didn't leave us much, but they left us the land and the mosquitoes and a few lessons about death and life."

"But, Abuelito," the boy asked, frowning, "you keep saying the Indians said such and such, but how do we know what they said? Who did they tell?"

"Well," Gabriel answered, taking the question seriously, thinking this is a boy who won't let the world swallow him without warning, he'll always be looking over his shoulder to see if the devil is approaching along the horizon. "Well, I suppose the Indians were no different from anybody else. Probably while their stomachs were being sliced open, they kept themselves alive just long enough to pass along a few stories to the men who killed them. And the killers, being no different from anybody else, must have just barely listened. And a few of them remembered, exchanging tales with men whose food was spilling onto the ground, it must have been something they couldn't possibly forget. Yes, I suppose after that a few of them must have remembered their own beliefs too," Gabriel added, thinking about good spirits battling evil.

———— ⌇ ————

"He won't be able to hide the sun with one finger," Miguelito predicted with satisfaction. "Here everyone is bitter. There will be blood and vengeance. Here each person will want revenge for something a neighbor did or said, for being turned in to the secret police for this or that ridiculous little thing. Some will want revenge because they are jealous of a neighbor who has a little more of this or that. Myself, I would have liked a chance to learn to drive. I would have liked to drive to one of the nice beaches when I have a vacation, to Playas del Este or Varadero. Instead I have to wait so long for so many different *guaguas*, with so many transfers, that by the time I get there it's time to turn around and start the return trip. You know I can't just take a taxi the way you do. Those are only for tourists, only with dollars. The taxis Cubans are allowed to take come very rarely and, when they do, you have to find one that's going in the direction you want to travel. You can't just get in and say take me here or there, you have to go wherever the taxi has its regular route.

"It bothers me very much that only members of the Party have a chance to learn to drive and to own a car. You say you're going on to visit other cousins but I say watch out for the ones who own cars because you never know, they must be members of the Party or they wouldn't be able to have cars and, with members of the Party you can never tell, you can never be sure. You can't talk freely or be yourself in front of them.

"No one would dare harm you since you are a foreigner. They would not dare harm one hair of your head, but me, us, well, you can imagine. I am afraid it will be a bloodbath when everyone finally has a chance to take revenge against the neighbors who have turned them in to be arrested and tortured."

Miguelito's beautiful wife sailed past us chasing her son. "We're afraid," she called over her shoulder. "We're afraid!"

I went back to Miguelito's house often. Aurora confided that she'd
been ordered not to return to work for a long time after the birth of her
child because the government could no longer afford to feed all the children in daycare centers, and there was no medicine for him in case he fell
ill. Miguelito said he was unhappy with his work, even though it required
technical skills and was considered useful. He wanted nothing more nor
less than the chance to write his own songs. All over Cuba, people were
getting into trouble for their words, yet, Miguelito sighed, he felt com-
pelled to let his songs emerge.

"Do you know the funniest thing that has happened in Cuba through
all of this?" he asked me as we sat in his father's shadowy room, surrounded
by the wings and talons of invisible warriors.

"Not too long ago, in a movie theater, some young people started
humming the words of a popular song when the Maximum Leader's face
appeared on the screen. 'This man is crazy,' they sang, 'he thinks he rules
the world.'"

My cousin chuckled, adding, "In Cuba it is a popular song. Somehow
the writer has gotten away with it, and the singers too. And the teenagers
who sang it were not really punished either, although it nearly started a
riot. That's the value of music here, because Cuba has always been full of
these same two things, slavery and music, injustice and music, cruelty and
music, tyranny and music.

"Other songwriters have managed too. There's one about William
Tell's son getting tired of having an apple on his head."

I hadn't come to my ancestors' homeland with any intentions of discussing politics. I hadn't expected anyone to talk about Fidel. I'd thought it
would be too dangerous, even if his name was never mentioned. When a
Cuban says he, in that certain roundabout way, everyone knows who is
being discussed. Even the exiles say he instead of naming the Maximum
Leader, as if the secret police were still listening, as if there could be no
safety, even in Coral Gables, Florida or Elizabeth, New Jersey.

Now, embroiled in my cousin's emotions and surrounded by his music, I
couldn't help developing that same deeply personal resentment against Fidel.
How profoundly he had wounded my family! He was even in the room,
behind closed doors, listening from behind the door. He was even deciding
which of Miguelito's songs he could dare to sing in a neighborhood
bristling with the pointed ears of spies. He had destroyed faith and trust
and love. On his island skeptics were pariahs and the outspoken were con-

demned to dungeons. The teenagers were right when they sang, 'This man is crazy.' Already he seemed to be turning into a crazed beast, wandering, I imagined, through a wilderness beyond sanity, eating grass, growing feathers and claws.

"If there is anything that has truly been collectivized in Cuba," Miguelito said quietly, "it is insanity."

Startled, I remained silent. Yes, insanity was contagious, like suicide. And Fidel had sworn that he would take the island to its death before he would see it retreat from his chosen path. He had said he would rather see Cuba sink beneath the sea. During the early years of the revolution he and his comrade Ché Guevara had announced the creation of a "New Man," a socialist man who would sacrifice himself for the good of his community. The words were noble and passionate, and the people were caught up by the illusion of him as their creator but, here they were, still people, and he was still leading them, but now was he leading them into oblivion, into a collective suicide. He was telling them to survive without food. He was asking them to join him in shouting, "Socialism or death!" Suddenly I felt a wave of relief as I decided that he might be more likely to commit some form of disguised suicide than Miguelito, so full of melodies and words.

Miguelito's songs were all unwritten ones, like the songs of gypsy troubadours who came to Cuba to escape the Spanish Inquisition. I believed Miguelito when he said he was very careful. There would not be a scrap of handwritten paper in his house. All the songs would be confined to his mind, trying to burst forth. A neighbor could turn him in to the secret police and, if they came in the early hours before dawn, tearing apart furniture and pillowcases, mattresses and books and clothes, all they would find was the energy flowing through his house, taking on form and sound, becoming visions of palm trees in the arms of ballerinas, of drums in mountain villages, dancers in golden caverns washed by waterfalls and light.

Then, just as I was deciding that everything would turn out well and that my cousin would be kept safe by his own passion and the angels battling throughout his house, he turned to face me and requested very seriously, very hopefully, "Tell me what people think of him over there."

When I was a child, with memories of Gabriel's farm still fresh and overflowing, adults would often say that they detected a perpetual sadness in my eyes. They accused me of carrying some unexplained sense of deep hidden tragedy. They said I seemed to wrap myself in a cloak of unreality. It was true. The unreality was real. Not long after my ninth birthday,

Gabriel was arrested and his entire family vanished. The farm was gone, along with all the cattle and horses.

Then the Missile Crisis came along, and my teacher warned the class, "If you see a brilliant white light approaching in the sky, it's not a meteor but an atomic bomb sent from an evil place, a place called Cuba, sent to destroy us all. You must hide under your desks, like this, crouched down in fetal position, with your hands protecting your head."

Neighbors were stockpiling canned foods. People were discussing the locations of basements that could serve as bomb shelters. For the first time in their lives, every person of every faith seemed to agree that the world would soon end.

Now here was my cousin, filled with his own decades of anguish, silenced by his homeland's collective fear and he was asking me whether the *Yanquis* cared about Cuba. I thought of all the opinions I had read by various experts. One commentator had written that Cuba could sink into the ocean and nobody would notice. After recovering from the panic of waiting for a nuclear attack that never came, most northerners seemed content to let Cuba continue to orbit outside their own realm of existence. No one needed the menacing alligator-shaped island. Cane sugar had been replaced by beet sugar and artificial sweeteners. The *conga*, *mambo* and *cha-cha-cha* had given way first to rock-and-roll, then disco, and now rap. Before my current pilgrimage to the island, I had mentioned to a few friends that I was going to Cuba to tell my relatives they were not forgotten. People had stared at me as if I had said I was going to the moon to plant flowers in the craters.

"Many in the North still believe Fidel is a heroic liberator who brought free education and free medicine to oppressed peasants who continue to worship him," I answered my cousin's question. "They say he's charismatic, has popular support. They say he's a father figure to all Cubans."

Miguelito shook his head and turned his face away so that I couldn't see his eyes.

"Others think he's crazy," I went on, trying to remember all the opinions I had heard about the Maximum Leader.

Miguelito faced me again. He looked despondent. Perhaps he had been hoping to hear that we in the powerful North still considered him a venomous enemy, that we were determined to destroy him and free his tyrannized people.

I felt like I had crossed through a time zone into a primitive world where millions of people could be trapped by the mysterious curse of a wizard. I would not have been surprised to look outside and see that I had landed in a medieval kingdom, where knights in armor chased fire-breathing dragons.

I continued, repeating everything I had ever heard about Fidel, that he was a megalomaniac, demented like Stalin, obsessed with his own ego and yet somehow able to convince crazed masses to assist him in his efforts to control them.

I remembered how Amparo had told me that in the early days after the revolution, when Batista's men were brought into the streets, the people would gather around them shouting, *"¡Al paredón, al paredón!'* It meant "To the firing squad!" The *paredón* was the "the big wall," the wall where executions were carried out, the walls of fortresses and castles.

"The terrible thing about it," my grandma had confessed, "was that those new executions were conducted without real trials, just like the executions carried out by the old tyrant we had all been fighting to get rid of. It was like the whole island was crazy, everyone sharing the same hallucination, seeing something that wasn't really there."

"And there are some, especially among the exiles," I told my cousin, "who believe Fidel received power through a contract with Satan."

Miguelito looked like he might laugh, but then his head drooped and he said, "Well, here there used to be some who thought that. They believed he had some sort of power through *santería*, you know *santería*, right? It's the Cuban form of voodoo."

I nodded. Yes, I knew *santería*.. In New York and Miami there were frequently tales about someone arrested for sacrificing farm animals inside city limits. There were exiles who dressed all in white and believed they could become saints by performing strange rituals.

When I was little, I used to hear adults saying that in Cuba even the trees could dance. The people, I heard, were like whirlwinds, twirling and shaking, all melody and passion and drumbeats, hurricane and stormy sea. But I couldn't imagine the Maximum Leader dancing! Certainly not dancing freely enough to become the horse ridden by a spirit good or evil. No, he seemed too desolate and cold, too rigid, sullen and stern, too reptilian. Only his words could dance. Maybe words were enough.

Miguelito said most of the *santeros* in Cuba no longer believed Fidel was a sorcerer. "The *santeros* say if he'd gotten power from the spirits, it would have been taken back by now, the spirits would have rebelled."

But I wasn't so sure. Cuba did seem like a cult. If he was a sorcerer, or even if he had been at one time, the profusion of demons would make sense. Because once they appeared on earth, riding the horse-forms of dancers, those spirits couldn't easily be sent away.

The last thing I said to my cousin about him was a quote from an article by Robert Cox, a journalist who lived in Argentina during the terrible times when Argentine mothers were trying to find out what had become of their "disappeared" sons and daughters. Cox later became a human rights activist and traveled to Cuba in 1990 as part of a United Nations investigative team. Finding repression in Cuba even more severe than in Argentina during the brutal era of the *desaparecidos*, Cox wrote, "It is possible to do more for Cuba's human rights heroes than pray, but praying for them is not a bad idea."

I returned to Miguelito's somber hideaway many times, for many conversations about the island and the North, but we no longer discussed suicide or the Maximum Leader. We listened to all the varied styles of music, spinning visions of dancers, butterflies, mountains, thatched huts, tranquil beaches and a distant, placid countryside.

I told my cousin about a group of young men I kept encountering in the tourist zones of Havana and the beach towns. They quietly called themselves "Singers to Cuba," and apparently they had been traveling all over the island asking people to sing.

"Last Sunday I went to church in one of the suburbs of Havana," I told Miguelito, since he seemed fascinated by anything outside his own four walls. "I just happened to be riding by on a *guagua*, and when it stopped in front of the church and a lot of people got out, I followed them." I wouldn't have guessed it was a church at all. It was just four walls with a floor and a ceiling. No altars, no stained glass, no decorations of any sort except for a mural of a typical Cuban landscape, a background of royal palms sprinkled across green hills, cane fields, a brilliant blue sky with rolling black storm clouds, and a full river rushing toward a waterfall in the foreground.

On the wall above the mural, words were written in big block letters, 'For God so loved the world...' and there were lots of people in the church, especially teenagers; in fact there was such a crowd that some of the teenagers had to stay outside and look in through a few square windows with vertical iron bars. They were teenagers raised as atheists. Seeing them gazing into the church through those barred windows, I immediately began to think of Cuba's little churches as stripped-bare places, like deserts, filled with what remains of a people after they've been shredded down to nothing but hope, after they've lost all property and status. The people were singing words like "Lord, illuminate Cuba" and "Renew me, Lord Jesus, I don't want to be the same anymore."

When the singing finally ended, most of the people were crying. The pastor said, "Which among you would like to come forward?" and one by one every Cuban in the church moved forward until the pews were empty, and the people all stood gathered around, holding hands and once again, spontaneously singing, "Here we are united again, something beautiful is going to happen."

And then all those young Cubans waved their hands toward heaven, and prayed for the island, and they even prayed for Fidel singing, "Illuminate our paths, and the path of the president."

And I told Miguelito how I'd left the little church feeling convinced that singing to Cuba was still a promising cause, despite everything, and how one of the teenagers followed me down the street, telling me that during the worst years all the Cuban pastors had spent many years in forced labor camps as punishment for singing. We talked about how the words of a popular Gloria Estefan song that speaks of coming "Into the light" seemed meaningful at the level of nations as well as individuals. The singer, a beautiful young Cuban exile, broke her back in a car accident and when she recovered, she returned to her career singing that "Starting again is part of the plan."

My cousin and I went on finding examples of inspiration by poets and singers. "Nobody knows you. No. But I sing to you," I quoted from the poem called "Absent Soul" by Federico García Lorca, a rebellious Spaniard who'd visited Cuba many decades ago.

"Blessed are those whose lives unfold in wings," Miguelito quoted the same poet, from a poem about caterpillars and butterflies. I was reminded of my arrival in Cuba in 1960, when I stepped off the airplane in Havana, an eight-year-old carrying a shoebox full of smuggled pet caterpillars which had already pupated. As I walked across the tarmac, I opened the box, and found that during the journey, my pets had been transformed from cocoons into butterflies, an assortment of startling yellow-striped tiger swallowtails, brilliant red monarchs and velvety black mourning cloaks. I told my cousin about the revelation, and how I was so surprised by the transformation that I stood outside the airplane, holding the box open until all the winged insects escaped into Cuba's sky.

"Even though we know what to expect of cocoons," Miguelito

answered, "we are always like children, still surprised."

——✺——

On the morning of Gabriel's arrest he led his inquisitive grandson down to the river. Despite its familiarity, Gabriel thought the river was still beautiful beyond belief, a river which took the breath away, a deep teal green river, reflecting the graceful royal palms with their silvery trunks and plumed tops. Thickets of vegetation cascaded down the banks to the warm glistening surface of the water. Beyond the river there were the dark forms of the Sierra de Escambray, the mountains looming close, yet distant, inexplicably out of reach, like something viewed through a mirror.

Gabriel took the opportunity to teach Taíno the names of a few of the plants, and to load the boy with advice in case he ended up like Gabriel's cousins, fighting in the mountains before he was even old enough to marry.

After he taught the boy which leaves could be used to heal wounds and soothe mosquito bites, Gabriel's thoughts wandered back to his own sons and daughters. One of the boys had married his first cousin, and then one of the girls had married another cousin. At first everyone had seemed happy living in the same thatched house, the way people do on farms. Eventually there came a quiet morning, before dawn, when the boy decided to go back to the house before the milking was done, and he found his sister's husband in the wrong bed. A great turmoil followed, and both marriages broke up. Gabriel's son started over with another wife from an unrelated family, and Gabriel's daughter started over with a new husband from a distant town. Now they all had their children, among them Taíno, and they all managed to live together in one small house, but soon it would be necessary to build new houses for the young families. Gabriel hoped each new house would have its own stone floor.

Gabriel and Taíno sat together on a damp ceiba log which had tumbled halfway down the river bank. He and his grandson reminisced about the feast they'd had in town on New Year's Day of the previous year, when everyone got together to celebrate Fidel's victory. What elation there had been. Alvaro and his brothers were among the revolutionary heroes, bearded and triumphant! There hadn't been so much joy in Cuba since the overthrow of Machado. Gabriel told Taíno about Daniel hiding under the big ceiba tree, and about Miguel singing to inspire the rebels.

"Of course, he didn't say he was singing to inspire them. He said he was singing because they inspired him."

———— ✺ ————

When I dressed like a foreigner and stayed inside the tourist zone, official guides watched my movements closely. Hotel maids, waitresses and taxi drivers made incessant inquiries about my solitary activities. Yet I found that if I dressed like a Cuban and spoke like a Cuban, remaining stoically silent most of the time, speaking to strangers only when necessary, and addressing them as comrade when I did, then I would be watched even more carefully, by the ubiquitous men in *guayaberas* who stood on every street corner, flanked every ration line, and rode every *guagua*, monitoring the sporadic whispered conversations.

I decided I was best off dressing like a tourist when alone and like a Cuban when accompanied by relatives. Although officially I was prohibited from visiting relatives, and officially my cousins were denied the right to speak to foreigners, I found that every cousin I visited expressed a strong desire to behave like ordinary families in ordinary places, going out in public together, walking and talking together as if the absurd array of small deranged laws did not exist.

Miguelito, more than any of the others, loved to walk up and down the streets of Old Havana with me, pointing out historical sites and discussing our lives just as if we were not taking any risk by being seen together. When he wanted to go out, Aurora made him carry my wedding picture in his pocket, with the letter *Abuelita* Amparo had written when she sent it, to prove we were really cousins and not just a heretofore quiet dissident, finally bursting, speaking openly to a foreigner.

Miguelito sometimes sang as we walked. He sang about a marble house which crumbled while its residents were asleep. Both ceiling and floor caved in, and a woman, still reclining on her bed, told the neighbors that at first she thought it was just a dream but when she woke up, her leg was broken, and she could see the sky. Aurora had assured me that all of

Miguelito's songs were true, taken from the seemingly impossible things which, in Cuba, she laughed, happen every day.

He sang about a poet who lived alone in a house by the sea. A storm carried away one half of his house, taking with it his typewriter and his entire library, leaving him to dwell in the other half, still writing about the sunset and the sea, while waves came swirling about his feet, coming in through the gap where once there had been a wall.

Sometimes, before going out, Miguelito would hang a big antique silver crucifix around his neck. It was the kind of jewelry Cubans were not supposed to have kept after the revolution. Soon after the Maximum Leader took control of the island, its inhabitants had been ordered to turn in all their guns, money, jewelry and other valuables, so that everyone could start over with nothing. Nearly everyone gave up their firearms, but even the most dedicated communist bureaucrats buried their valuables rather than turn them over. Now, with the economy collapsing, the government was luring the heirlooms and jewelry out of hiding by allowing Cubans to sell hoarded valuables in exchange for shopping privileges in otherwise prohibited dollar stores.

When Miguelito wore his big silver crucifix, he looked like a foreigner, like a lean moustached cowboy from nineteenth-century Texas or Mexico. He left the top button of his shirt open to make sure the crucifix showed, and he walked with pride, relieved to be taking a step so bold and defiant. He told me that as a Cuban, wearing a crucifix in public could brand him as a second class citizen, faithful in a land still officially atheistic. Within his own neighborhood, he was taking a risk. In the tourist zone, he felt anonymous and spoke freely of the elation he felt when disregarding the usual elaborate code of conduct.

When Miguelito, with his crucifix, and I, with my foreign clothes and camera bag, walked through Old Havana together, we both felt safe. When we rode the beet-and-mustard striped *guagua*, we knew we were, like all Cubans, vulnerable. Few tourists braved the crowds and heat of the Cuban *guagua*. Most confined themselves to Tourist-Taxis and air conditioned tour buses. In the *guagua* Miguelito and I stood out as the only people daring to converse. My cousin was so tired of silence that even on a crowded *guagua*, he would lean his head down toward the window and say without lowering his voice, "This is all I have ever known. In my entire life, this is all I have ever seen." People would look away, pretending they hadn't heard.

With a sweep of his hand he would indicate everything beyond the window, decaying marble houses, winged statues, hordes of young men on bicycles, the sea wall, the harbor, El Morro Castle. When the *guagua* passed La Cabaña Fortress, I was relieved to see my cousin remain quiet. No matter how much he wanted to point out the dungeons, such overt defiance would be foolish.

I looked out at the tourists snapping photographs of each other standing next to the cannons. I couldn't help thinking of all the names I read each month, when my human rights bulletins arrived, of men arrested for joining a movement of artists seeking freedom of expression, and human rights monitors arrested by State Security, held without charge.

On the *guagua*, surrounded by silent Cubans, Miguelito went on asking questions about the U.S., my family, my friends, my life. He asked about my schooling, my wedding, about jobs, vacations, grocery shopping. He asked about childbirth and books, movies and music. He asked about rhythm-and-blues singers, and about the irrigated orchards near my arid northern home, and about the coyotes which roamed the orchards hunting jackrabbits, roadrunners and ground squirrels. We rode many different *guaguas* along many different routes, past Revolution Square with its tanks and armed guards, past a colonial cemetery with its magnificent variety of carved angels, past an enormous white monument to José Martí, and the towering Soviet Embassy, a skyscraper which pierces the Cuban sky with its listening apparatus for spying on U.S. communications systems. Miguelito named the landmarks as we passed them. I didn't want my cousin to keep taking chances, so I asked if we could get out and walk.

The streets of Havana were filling with tourists as Cuba prepared to host the Pan American Games. Tourists from Europe and Latin America were flooding the hotel zone and the secret police could hardly keep up with their massive efforts to monitor the movements of Cubans and insure that they didn't violate the rule against speaking to foreigners. The Neighborhood Committees were being trained as riot squads. In every crowd of Cubans, police informers were planted to disrupt any incipient protest through Acts of Repudiation, by mobilizing groups of citizens to surround and beat anyone who openly voiced discontent.

Descriptions of Acts of Repudiation came in the monthly human rights bulletins. Committee members surround the house of a dissident or they surround him on the streets. They chant slogans and create the appearance of a spontaneous pro-government demonstration. The Act of Repudiation can go on for hours or it might end abruptly with the arrest of its target. Sometimes the dissident's house is ransacked. Family members and visitors may be held captive inside the house. Acts of Repudiation are effective because they instill in the dissident a fear of isolation, creating the illusion that only he and his family are unhappy with a system loved by multitudes. The Act of Repudiation is designed to stimulate a wave of self-doubt and to terrify bystanders who swear they will never speak out and place their own families in such a precarious position.

Miguelito and I had just emerged from a *guagua*. The afternoon sky had suddenly clouded over and a light rain was beginning to fall. As we walked, we found ourselves surrounded by blue-uniformed civil police. Miguelito kept right on talking and gradually the blue uniforms drifted away. Soldiers replaced them. Again we were surrounded. Still, my cousin kept talking. The cluster of soldiers walked beside us, behind us, and in front. I counted fourteen of them.

Looking beyond them, at the crumbling walls, I noticed a small red cross and a child's handprint, the only graffiti I had seen since arriving in Havana. I felt like someone discovering pictographs in a prehistoric cave. They reminded me of a story by Reinaldo Arenas called "Singing From the Well," about a child who starts scribbling on tree trunks, sending his stern family into a flurry of accusations when they decide he is crazy.

I thought of Anacaona, the ten sisters who emerged as Cuba's first all-female singing group after three years of hiding inside their Havana house during the anarchy of Machado's overthrow in the early 1930's.

How many artists must now be waiting behind closed doors, practicing secretly, waiting for the day when they could come out of their houses, singing and dancing!

I withdrew the camera from my bag and began fussing with the lens as I walked. Then I started snapping photographs of the soldiers. One of them waved his semiautomatic weapon at me in a threatening gesture that meant stop. I smiled and turned the camera toward the broken walls of the houses around me. I pointed the lens up toward the roofless apex and disintegrating columns of a once-elegant building that looked like the ruined remains of some ancient Greek temple.

Beside me, Miguelito was smiling, looking as fearless and confident as any newly-arrived foreigner still unaware of the vast network of vigilant guides, secret police and informers. The soldiers glanced at each of us, then at each other. They shrugged, grinning, and moved away, pursuing some young Cuban women who had begun to flirt with them. Soon they were

walking far ahead of us, surrounding the girls, who were laughing and con-
versing with them in loud fast voices, still sounding as I remembered from
1960, raucous and musical, like wild parrots joined by small song birds as
they all fed from the same fruit tree.

On the morning of his arrest Gabriel told Taíno about the long struggle for independence from Imperial Spain, about the Mambí rebels who
hid in the caves and mountains and ventured out to ambush Spanish
troops with the advantage of surprise, firing from the tops of royal palms
or from horseback as their daring mounts charged out of the brush.
Gabriel told Taíno that the Mambises were such good horsemen that
their generals were sometimes referred to as Centaurs, and the women
who fought with them came to be called Amazons by the foreign press, so
ferociously did they wield their horn-handled machetes against Spanish
bayonets. Gabriel told Taíno that some of the Mambises started as slaves,
freed for the purpose of fighting, while others started as plantation own-
ers, burning their own cane fields to cripple the colonial economy.
Gabriel told his grandson that many of the laws passed by Spain were
ridiculous petty restrictions no one could hope to obey, that Cuban men
and boys over the age of fifteen were to be shot on sight if they left their
homes for any reason and bohíos not flying white flags were to be burned.
    "Famine and yellow fever swept across the island," Gabriel told his
grandson, reminding the boy that during those terrible years Taíno's
great-grandmother had been a guajirita just starting out in life, searching
for hope and love.
    "In Havana there was nothing to eat, absolutely nothing. Children,
it was said, had to rummage through the waste that fell from the rear
ends of horses, collecting undigested grain from the manure. In the
countryside, people ate the rotting corpses of livestock killed by the
Spaniards to prevent them from reaching the mouths of the rebels. The
dungeons of El Morro Castle were spilling over with Cuban blood, and
poems were being written on the walls of each cell by men who knew
they would never again see sunlight or blue sky. That is the part you
have to remember, Taíno, that even though they knew no one else

would ever read those poems except for the next group of prisoners, those men trapped in darkness kept finding passionate words of hope."

We walked through the tourist zone of Old Havana, until we came to a makeshift booth set out on the sidewalk, under a protective thatched awning. An old man sat on a stool behind the booth, demonstrating the preparation of tobacco leaves and the rolling of cigars. He looked dignified. Like many of the older Cuban men, he wore a *guayabera*, embroidered shirts by now I associated with plainclothes policemen even though they were so commonly in use. The cigarmaking booth was decorated with a colorful alligator-shaped map of Cuba, showing the island's most famous tobacco growing regions. Around the edges of the booth, cedar boxes were opened to display the various shapes, sizes and colors of cigars. A brochure explained in Spanish, English, Russian, French, Japanese, Italian and German that cigars were an invention of the peaceful Cuban Indians, who attributed spiritual and medicinal properties to the large, floppy leaves of native tobacco.

The old man's expression was somber. I was still a little nervous from our incident with the police and soldiers. I kept wondering what might have happened if we hadn't managed to convince them that we were just tourists out for a stroll, taking pictures despite the rain. My photographs of the crumbling buildings actually seemed to embarass the soldiers, who were young and must have longed to feel proud of the island they were being trained to protect.

Immensely relieved to be free of our spontaneous military escort, Miguelito and I were now chattering like true foreigners. The old man glanced up at us, his eyes reflecting a mixture of envy and resentment. I felt sorry for him, working alone to entertain the tourists. Traditionally, he would have been rolling his cigars in a factory, surrounded by colleagues and entertained by a reader selected for the power and dramatic impact of his voice. Since colonial times, Cuban cigar workers had been chipping in a portion of their salaries to hire a reader who could carry them, with his booming voice, into the realm of classic novels, poetry and world news. The cigarmakers voted to decide which stories they wanted to hear: *Don*

Quixote de la Mancha, *A Tale of Two Cities*, *The Count of Monte Cristo*. From knights in armor and deeds of courage in faraway lands, the cigar-makers, as time passed, progressed to the poetry of José María de Heredia and José Martí, both exiled from their native Cuba for conspiring against the domination of Imperial Spain.

Watching the solitary old man at work, a line from Heredia's verse came to me, "Dreams—Dreams! I am an exile, and for me there is no country and there is no love." The old man seemed confined to some form of invisible exile, dwelling silently in his own land, like someone wandering through a dream. I gazed at the map of Cuba's tobacco growing regions. Most were in Pinar del Río Province, on the far western tip of the alligator's tail.

Miguelito watched the old man as I bent to study the map. Suddenly, my cousin reached down from his greater height and ran one finger across the tail of the reptile-shaped map. In his own voice, without whispering, he said, "That is where Gabriel's sons live." I looked up at my cousin's face and he nodded grimly, as if to assure me that he knew what I was thinking.

A small girl, smiling shyly, came sidling up to the old cigarmaker. He turned to smile at her, saying "My little granddaughter." She put her arm around his neck, and started singing. Suddenly the old man no longer seemed to be in exile. The child smiled at me. I tugged at Miguelito's arm, and pulled him away from the booth just as a cluster of German tourists approached.

Miguelito's words had affected me more deeply than anything else he had said about Cuba. Overcome by an urgency, by the need to know more, I led my cousin toward the Malecón, almost running to get away from the listening ears of so many strangers, both Cuban and foreign.

I had gone to Cuba planning to visit my relatives without compromising their safety. I had gone with the determination that of all topics, the one which could not be discussed was Gabriel. Now Miguelito had swept away that barrier by mentioning our lost cousins, the grown boys I remembered so well from that summer on Gabriel's farm when I followed his sons every morning before dawn from the thatched *bohío* to the corral, crossing a morass of sticky red mud, going barefoot even though I had been warned that worms from the soil could crawl up through my insides and consume me.

We hurried toward the sea wall. Memories of Gabriel's farm came sweeping through me, hot, fertile, intense, Gabriel on a horse, his sons rounding up cattle, the river reflecting a tumble of vegetation.

We walked along the wall constructed to confine the sea to its boundaries during storms, a hopeless task on an island where storms can make winged statues fly and transform the fronds of palms into blades as keen as *machetes*. We found a deserted portion of the long curving wall, short on the street side, crumbling along the top, precipitous on the side facing the ocean. We sat with our legs dangling over the edge, watching the sea, the clearing sky, the angular black frigate birds circling over El Morro Castle. Miguelito didn't ask why I had rushed him away from the tourist zone. Instead, he started singing, softly at first, then louder and finally, at the top of his voice, attracting appreciative glances from the small groups of silent people seated all along the sea wall, people who seemed to be waiting patiently for something they had been expecting for centuries.

Miguelito was singing about El Morro Castle and the poems written inside, on dungeon walls. He made the song sound like it referred to a time long ago, to the long rebellion against Spain. I hushed him.

He smiled, knowing he had managed to set a few minds wondering. I hoped the minds were not those of police informers. "Tell me about Gabriel's sons," I whispered. They were Miguelito's first cousins, my second cousins. They were, as far as I knew, people who seemed to have never existed, except within the boundaries of my memory. Gabriel's sons seemed to have been swallowed by time and distance. No one in New York or Miami knew what became of them after Gabriel's arrest or, if they knew, they wouldn't say, wouldn't talk, afraid to open an old wound.

"You were there in 1960?" Miguelito asked.

I nodded. "After the revolution," I said, "but before the Missile Crisis."

"Well, you know, then, about the fighting in the mountains?"

I shook my head.

"Already, in 1960, when you were there, and I remember seeing you there, with your pet spiders and scorpions, already there were *Alzados* in the mountains then, just a few leagues from Gabriel's farm. My father said he believes Gabriel didn't even know much about it himself. No one was sure what was happening in those mountains, but everyone knew that when Cubans are ready to rise up against injustice, they start by going up into the mountains. *Se alzan*, they rise up. That's how the *Mambí* warriors started when they hid in the mountains, in the wilderness, to fight against the soldiers of the King of Spain. That's how Fidel started when he rose up against Batista.

"But the world didn't know about this war which was already going on up there in the mountains, right above our heads, while we were just little children playing with farm animals and chasing each other around the pastures.

"I believe the world still knows very little about this. It was a war which has been kept almost entirely hidden. It lasted from 1960 to 1966. The people who rose in arms against Fidel during that forgotten war were simple peasants, *guajiros*, just like Gabriel. Their leaders were the very officers who led Fidel's own troops to victory in 1959, only a year earlier. But when they saw that he was consolidating power for himself instead of for the people, they rebelled. They had barely set down their guns from the last war, so it was easy to take them up again and just keep fighting. The *guajiros* were the very same people who fed Fidel's troops when they were hungry, nursed them when they were wounded and sent their own sons to die for a noble and passionate cause; the very peasants Fidel had promised to help, to defend against the foreign sugar monopolies. Only when the farmers became enlightened about the direction of the revolution under him, the way he was turning his back on them and planning to take their little patches of land away, to collectivize, they rose up in arms again, for another war. Only this time they lost, and this time the war became a terrifying secret.

Miguelito was speaking very quietly. People drifting along the sea wall could not hear him over the incantations of the sea and a whispering breeze. I felt immensely relieved to finally hear even a small portion of the truth about Gabriel and his family. I felt shadowed by the fiery wings of angels. There was, after all, an explanation for the sense of unreality I always experienced whenever I thought of my great-uncle and his farm.

Miguelito could tell me very little about that secret war and Gabriel's arrest. Even within Cuba, he explained, most of the details remain unknown or unspoken or misrepresented as a campaign against banditry.

"They hunted down the *Alzados* one by one, and buried their bodies in mass graves in the mountains. He called it the *Lucha Contra Bandidos*, the struggle against bandits. He said it was a crackdown on crime in the mountains but what is there to steal up there? Nothing but peasants and coffee trees and wild animals. There were no bandits.

"What was done to those people was a horror. Not so much the *Alzados*, because they were fighting, and when you fight you take your chances, but the *guajiros* who never did anything but work the land every day of their lives. Men like Gabriel were not part of that war. They were down at the foot of the mountains, in the hills, working just like they always worked, making food emerge from the soil."

Miguelito looked up toward a raft of dark storm clouds blowing away across the sea. "I don't know much about it," he concluded, "but I believe our uncle Daniel does. To find out more about El Pueblo Cautivo, The Captive Towns, you must ask Daniel. They released Gabriel from prison right before his death but they wouldn't let him go to live with his family in El Pueblo Cautivo. There are quite a few Captive Towns, but theirs is the one called Ciudad Sandino, in Pinar del Río Province, the place I showed you on the map, a tobacco growing region. Some of the best cigars are made there, the ones Cuba exports to Europe and other places. When they released Gabriel, they let him go to Daniel's house to die but they wouldn't allow him to live with his wife and family in El Pueblo Cautivo, and he was never allowed to return to the farm, or even to Trinidad. Pinar del Río is a tourist area now. Fishing lakes, hunting reserves, the mogotes with their caves, cigar factory tours. Very few outsiders realize that the province is riddled with captive towns and forced labor camps."

Silent now, I considered everything I knew about Pinar del Río. The mogotes were limestone bluffs, curious features of karst topography, forested knobs rising up out of the land, bordered by sheer cliffs and underlain by vast networks of limestone caves, caverns which had once served as a last refuge for the island's besieged Indians.

"Where did they take Gabriel?" I asked. "To which prison?"

"Boniato, I think," Miguelito answered sorrowfully. Then he began to hum, and by the time I'd absorbed the shock of hearing that my beloved great-uncle had been sent to Cuba's most notorious political prison, my cousin was again singing but this time his words were nostalgic ones, a wistful guajiro melody about floating down through the sky to a river where sharks chased mermaids in from the sea.

Gazing toward El Morro Castle, I listened and, when Miguelito's impromptu song ended, he said, "Your turn now," and I realized he was playing one of the games guajiros play at guateque feasts, when they take turns racing horses and inventing new songs.

I felt too overpowered by emotion. How could I sing? How could I carry a tune or invent a verse now, while drowning under this flood of memory? Perhaps a quote borrowed from the verse of some other, more rebellious poet than myself, perhaps Federico García Lorca: "Poetry is the impossible made possible. A harp which has, in place of strings, hearts and flames."

Or the Chilean Gabriela Mistral, who named herself after a hot wind and wrote, "In the secret of night my prayer climbs like the liana...I cling to the vine of my prayer.

But the only poetry I really needed was the spontaneous verse of Gabriel and I had forgotten all his words and could only remember the sound of his voice and the rhythm of his horse's hoofs cantering as he sang.

On the morning of his arrest Gabriel looked into the river and felt overwhelmed by its apparent serenity, more estuary than mountain stream.

"Look how the palms resemble dancers," he beckoned to his grandson. "Sometimes when a shark chases a manatee this far upstream, you'd think you were looking into a story book."

When the boy didn't answer, Gabriel looked up. Taíno was sniffing the air. Gabriel turned away from the river to watch his grandson who was already learning guajiro hunting skills. "Death or fire?" he asked, smelling the answer himself and feeling his blood sinking inside his limbs.

"Both," Taíno responded.

Gabriel glanced one last time at the deep green water, streaked with sunlight and shadow. During hurricane season the banks of the river had been overrun with land crabs fleeing the storm. Splay-footed jacanas had come stepping across the water, moving from leaf to floating leaf, looking like small miracles rather than hungry birds.

How exhausted I am, Gabriel thought. How tiring is the fear of sleep when the soul needs rest. "Let's go," he called to Taíno, who was already far ahead of him, running up the bank, plunging through a tangle of vines and thorny acacias.

Gabriel ran behind his shrieking grandson and, long before he reached his flaming bohío, he saw a mass of billowing gray smoke rising from the thatched roof. By the time they reached the burning house, the towering cane field was also aflame and as Taíno approached, one of Gabriel's untamed cats came screeching out of the burning sugar, its tail wrapped in rags soaked with gasoline. Laughing as the burning cat emerged from a sea of smoldering cane, a reptile-uniformed soldier reached down and tossed Taíno up into the air, sending the boy sailing through empty sky into the back of a truck where all the other grandchildren were already cowering.

———— ∽ ————

Overwhelmed by Miguelito's brief description of the secret war which swallowed Gabriel and his family and the farm, livestock and all, I went about the business of seeking out other relatives in Havana, to tell them they were not forgotten. I felt foolish saying it, like someone trying to converse in rhyme but I felt that I had no choice. I promised Miguelito and Aurora I wouldn't leave the city without first saying goodbye to them but my time in Cuba was limited by the government tourist agency and, if I delayed much longer, I wouldn't have a chance to see Isabelita and her son Dieguito in Trinidad, or Daniel in his village on the remote northern shore of Oriente Province, on the head of the alligator, not far from Boniato prison, the nightmarish center of torture and brutality I had read about so often in my human rights bulletins.

Checking my list of distant cousins, I walked along the highway in front of my hotel until a Tourist-Taxi came along and took me to the distant outskirts of Havana where, Amparo had told me when I was compiling my list of relatives, some of her cousins lived. They were descendants of her uncle and his wife, the daughter of a Congolese slave. Amparo had told me that in the countryside near Trinidad, her aunt and uncle were among the happiest people she'd ever known, always joking and laughing, behaving as if they'd tricked the devil himself, even though groups of hostile children sometimes threw stones at them when they ventured into town. Her aunt used to go up into the mountains alone, collecting rare, fragrant blossoms, and bringing them into town to be sold to Spanish-born ladies who bought them through the iron bars of tall, colonial windows. The flowers were strangely shaped, long and feathery, like plumes, or round and silky like pincushions. By the time she told me about her aunt and uncle, Abuelita Amparo was ninety years old and had lived in New York for more than two decades. She couldn't remember the names of the flowers but she remembered their scents and textures, and the bouncing rainbow they made when her aunt carried them along Trinidad's cobblestone streets.

I had met Abuelita's cousins in 1960, when I was eight years old and they were already in their sixties. I didn't expect them to remember me.

At least this cabdriver was more cordial than the first. He took me past the crumbling houses of Havana's suburbs, past hundreds of winding ration lines and crowds of grim-faced silent people awaiting the sporadic departures of *guaguas* headed for the city. He pointed out the microbrigades, the high-rise Cuban equivalent of New York's dismal "projects." I knew there were *guajiros* who'd been judged counter-revolutionary because they'd refused to leave their ancestral palm-thatched *bohíos* for the anonymity of these communist tenements. The taxi driver asked about medical insurance and company cars, microwave ovens and videocassette recorders. He asked many of the same questions Miguelito and Aurora had asked, how many television channels did I have access to in the North, and how much did it cost to buy a car.

As I answered, my thoughts kept returning to my own questions, the ones I couldn't ask, about rebels in the mountains, and Captive Towns. I thought of Armando Valladares, whose letters and poems, written in prison and smuggled out, first alerted the world to Cuba's prison conditions. I wanted to ask about one of Fidel's own rebels, arrested in 1961 for retiring from the armed forces as a protest against the direction taken by the new government, sentenced to thirty years. And about the dissidents detained in 1988 in connection with the visit by a United Nations Human Rights Commission and again, in 1989, held without charge until 1990. I wondered about those arrested in1989 for reporting incidents of human rights abuses, charged with "dissemination of false news."

I wanted to ask about the men arrested in 1980 for attempting to seek asylum in the Papal nunciature, both sentenced to twenty-five years.

In Cuba, there was no one to ask. Those who could answer were imprisoned, or silenced by fear. I imagined the reaction I would get if I asked one of the pretty young *Cubatur* guides to tell me the history of the Captive Towns. I imagined asking for directions to the homes of Gabriel's sons in their Captive Town. I imagined daring to ask such forbidden questions and being sent to State Security Headquarters for one of the interrogations Cubans dreaded so intensely. I tried to decide which poems I would write on cell walls. I imagined being Cuban, belonging to Cuba.

"Do you have many apples over there?" the loquacious driver interrupted my bitter fantasy.

"Apples? Yes, very many," I answered, startled, intrigued by his query. In the U.S. I had often overheard older exiles reminiscing about apples. "Many different sizes, shapes and colors," I added. "Apples can be green or yellow, round or heart-shaped."

"I remember tasting apples at Christmas," the driver said, turning to smile at the memory. "Every year, my family bought one big red perfect imported apple. My father sliced it into many little pieces, and everybody got a taste, even the children."

The driver looked old enough to have tasted quite a few apples before the revolution, before the Maximum Leader decided to replace Christmas with "Revolution Day."

"In the U.S.," I said, "all the exiles old enough to remember apples talk about them at Christmas. Of course, there they can eat as many as they want, so it's different. They say it loses that flavor of luxury."

"How long it has been since I've seen one of those big red apples! Next time," the driver urged, "bring me one from across the sea when you come back here again in an airplane!"

Next time ! My mind caught the words and savored them. Would there be another time? Would another thirty-one years pass? Perhaps the next time I came to Cuba I would be an old woman. Despite the decaying stone houses and disintegrating economy, Fidel still had the power to make family reunions practically impossible.

"I haven't found this address yet," the driver called over his shoulder.

Seated alone in the back seat of the Soviet-built government taxi, I remembered that in Cuba you needed to know the cross streets if you wanted to find an address. By themselves, street numbers meant nothing to taxi drivers. I searched through my bag and came up with a note listing the cross streets near the address of each relative. The cab stopped in front of a crumbling concrete block wall, where an old man sat alone, waiting. Like everyone in Cuba, he seemed to be waiting for something intangible, invisible, something more than a crowded bus.

"Is it far to this street?" the driver asked, holding up the note. In Cuba, nearly everyone can read. Literacy was one of the few undeniable accomplishments of the revolution even though reading materials were severely limited by censorship.

The old man hopped off his wall and came forward, removing his withered straw hat from a shiny bald head and bending to look in the open window next to my seat. Speaking directly to me, he said, "For you it is not far. You have a taxi. For me it is far. I have only my feet." Replacing his hat, he chuckled. The driver and I joined in, laughing too. As the taxi pulled away from the curb, I waved to the old man, who had returned to his wall and was again sitting patiently, waiting.

"We have shortages," the driver said, "but humor is not one of them." I agreed, thinking of all the small disguised complaints I had heard Cubans conceal in wrappings of genuine amusement. No wonder one Cuban cartoonist had continued making fun of the government even though the result was imprisonment and five years detention in a State Security psychiatric ward for the criminally insane.

"We still make straw hats," the driver said after a pause, "like the one that old man was wearing but most of them are exported, like everything. Like the meat. Out in the countryside you'll see that we still have plenty of cattle and chickens but now, with the economic situation, everything is exported. The search for foreign currency! Sacrifice, they keep telling us. Working out in the hot sun without a hat, now that's sacrifice!"

Finally, the taxi arrived at the address we were seeking. As we turned onto the block, another old man stood waiting on the corner. This one approached the car rapidly, like a sentry. His expression was stern. He leaned against the taxi, pressing both hands to the metal of the door. Inspecting me, he demanded, "What are you doing here?"

Obviously, Tourist-Taxis were not common in this neighborhood. The suburb looked very poor. The streets were pocked by a scramble of potholes and flooded unfinished ditches. Chunks of broken asphalt lay on the surface like discarded scraps of thick black paper. As everywhere, there were people standing around, waiting. Some sat on the broken curb. Others clustered in small groups, barely speaking.

I assumed that my grandmother's cousins were much too old for dissidence. I couldn't imagine that women in their nineties would be subject to the same restrictions as the restless youth. Perhaps I should have reached the address by wading through a maze of bus transfers and botched directions. The maps given to tourists were incomplete or outdated. Like everything in Cuba, an unfamiliar location could be found only by spending great volumes of time.

I spoke the names of Amparo's cousins, deciding that for old women there should be little risk involved in receiving an unannounced guest from far away.

The old man studied me. "For twenty years," he announced with pride, "I have been the head of my block's Committee for the Defense of the Revolution and, never once, in all those years, have I heard these names or seen this address. With a look of intense satisfaction, he gave his verdict. *"No existen."* They do not exist. It was the same phrase I kept hearing all over Cuba, from official sources. Nothing existed, not the beggars who accosted tour buses, not the despair when ration lines ran out of bread, not the curiosity about life beyond the rough, knobby green skin of the alligator.

Just that morning, when I casually asked a guide about resentment against tourists who received more than they could eat at bountiful segregated restaurants where no Cubans were allowed, she had answered, with a look of disbelief, *"No existe.* In Cuba," she had insisted, casting a look of warning towards me, "bitterness does not exist. We are all a family here. We help each other."

Glancing out the taxi window, I now noticed that two old women were peering out at me from the house which bore the same address I carried on my note. From behind a faded blue curtain, they were looking out, perhaps wondering who I was and what I wanted in their neighborhood. I knew I had lost this round. These two relatives, for some incomprehensible official reason, could not be told they were not forgotten.

"This," the Committee leader said with finality, slicing the air with one hand to illustrate his decision, "is absolute." Suddenly I felt more Cuban than *Yanqui,* powerless, bursting with questions, but afraid to ask.

Sighing as the taxi pulled away from the proud committee chief, I raised one hand feebly in hypocritical thanks,

I was silent on the long taxi ride back to the hotel. When we arrived in front of the placid beach with its armed patrol, I thanked the driver and promised to bring apples on my next trip. Knowing I was lying, we both laughed.

I walked slowly toward my hotel room, which faced the sea. I switched on the television, with its two government-operated channels. On one I found a newscaster announcing a decision that had just been made by Fidel Castro Ruz, President of the Republic, president of the Council of Ministers and President of the Council of State. On the second channel there was a news brief about a ceremony attended by Fidel Castro Ruz, Commander-in-Chief of the Armed Forces. I felt like a child who had time-traveled into a science fiction story.

Clicking the Maximum Leader out of existence, I switched off the television and pulled open the drapes, revealing a brilliant sun glistening across the sea. Soldiers passed along the beach, black gun barrels standing out against the soft white sand. Uniformed policemen passed close to my window, patrolling the hotel grounds.

A maid approached my window, gesturing. "You are invited to an extravaganza," she said. "A show, Las Vegas-style." I locked my room and followed her out to a quiet walkway shadowed by cascades of red blossoms. "In Cuba," the maid said to me, quietly, "we don't talk much, but we have faith. You have to have faith," she repeated, "in something." I was left with the impression that whatever she had trusted in the past was now gone, and the faith was looking for a new direction. "You have relatives here, don't you?" she asked, watching my face carefully.

Taken aback, I hesitated. The name on her uniform was the same as my grandmother's, Amparo. It made me want to trust her, but potential complications flashed through my mind. If I told her the truth, openly admitting that I was a Cuban-American visiting relatives without permission from the government, I risked being deported. Amparo seemed to be awaiting my decision anxiously. She was probably just another Cuban wanting me to smuggle a letter to Miami or New Jersey. On the other hand, she could be State Security.

"Excuse me," I told Amparo, patting her on the arm and rushing away. When I turned to wave at her I caught one last glimpse of her crestfallen expression. I felt furious with the Maximum Leader for creating this absurd atmosphere of uncertainty and dissimulation.

I followed the walkway until, reaching the patio where gold-sequined musicians were playing for a troop of dancers in glittery string-bikinis. I sat under a golden shower of cassia flowers, at a round white table covered with yellow petals detached by wind. Instantly, a parasoled rum drink appeared in the hand of a smiling white-encased waiter. I accepted the drink, paying with dollars and receiving my change in tourist coins, a small heap of glittering silver orchids, hummingbirds and moon-snails. At first the dancers appeared nervous and awkward. When the music stopped, they circulated through the audience of Canadian businessmen and French scuba divers and soon I realized that they were letting the men know they were available after the show. The hotel, like everything else in Cuba, was owned and operated by the government. How odd I felt watching the once-puritanical revolution take on the role of official pimp. One of Fidel's promises had been an end to the pre-revolutionary gambling and prostitution *Yanqui* gangsters had introduced to the island during Prohibition, when affluent North Americans could easily sail to Cuba for the weekend.

I rose from the flower-littered table, leaving the tourist coins behind, feeling like someone in an underwater dream, walking in slow motion, flanked by strange creatures from beneath the sea. Since arriving in Havana my only contact with the outside world had been brief, cautious conversations with foreign tourists.

Twice I had tried to call home from a long-distance phone service operating out of the Hotel Habana Libre. Both times I had reached my husband's answering machine. Calls outside Cuba were monitored by State censors so I left brief cryptic messages and went on orbiting in this other reality, wondering from time to time whether the safe, predictable home I'd left behind could ever have existed, knowing my children and husband would be worried. Each morning, as I awakened in my hotel room, I passed through a moment of dread before remembering that the North was real too. The fear felt like a New York subway, dark, narrow, elongated, a winding serpent of tunnel-vision.

There was no point trying to write home. Censorship slowed the mail so drastically that each letter was delayed between one and two months. By the time a letter could reach home, I would have preceded it. As a teenager in New York, where Abuelita Amparo received letters from her sister Isabelita exactly twice each month, I had imagined the life of a censor, trying to figure out how he would be affected by the letters he read from mothers in Cuba to sons in Miami, and from sweethearts separated by exile.

Now I started to wonder whether revisiting Cuba had been a futile gesture.

What had I done to Miguelito? Now that he had gone out in public, speaking his mind and singing his verses, would he return to silence? I knew that somehow, by appearing out of nowhere, I had triggered the release of memories he could no longer confine. And on top of everything else, the room where he wrote his music was swarming with demons and angels.

In the morning, I decided, I would make one last attempt to call home before leaving Havana. In the countryside long-distance calls were likely to be impossible. After calling, I would try to visit one more distant cousin, say goodbye to Miguelito and Aurora, then set out for Trinidad to visit my great-aunt Isabelita and her son Dieguito. From there I would try to make my way to the remote village where Daniel, at eighty-six years of age, might be willing to tell me about Gabriel.

As a child I met my great-uncle Daniel only briefly, when he passed through the farm on his way to Havana from the eastern village which served as a base camp for his archaeological explorations of Taíno Indian artifacts and the remains of caves and hidden villages once inhabited by runaway slaves.

Daniel had told me that African-born slaves were much more likely to escape than their descendants born in captivity. After a few generations, he had said, survival in the wilderness must have seemed almost as frightening as the more familiar horrors of the plantations. People, Daniel explained, had a tendency to choose what was known.

———— ∽ ————

On the morning of Gabriel's release from the punishment cell, he recovered consciousness slowly, imperceptibly, like a person moving from one dream to another.

He was sure his eyes were open wide, but he could see nothing, perceive nothing. Only darkness, a blackness so ferocious, so absolute that Gabriel considered the possibility that he was already dead. Memories drifted into his mind as he struggled to recall the events leading up to his imprisonment. Nothing. Nothing of consequence had occurred. He had milked the cows, cantered across the land, finished a breakfast of corn meal and wandered down to the river with Taíno. Then the smoke, the cat with its tail flaming, and Taíno sailing through the air like a flying fish over the sea.

No risks. No contact with any Alzados, not even his own cousins had come down from the mountains asking for food. He didn't even know if it was true that they were in the mountains preparing another rebellion. But he had done nothing dangerous, nothing foolish, nothing, and now he didn't know whether days had passed in the darkness, or years. His wife, the children and babies?

"Never again in your entire life," someone had said. "Absolutely never will you see these farms again." Now Gabriel could recall the voice of the one who called himself the Instructor. A long journey in the back of a truck crammed with men, guajiros and Alzados, all thrown in together, but mostly just guajiros, all the men from all the neighboring farms, fathers, sons, cousins, nephews, all thrown in together with no place to vomit or urinate when the heat inside the truck became unbearable.

At night they had been taken out and herded into a shed on a military encampment. Noodle soup, that was the meal he had been given in the shed. All around him, men were receiving yellow rice with spiced meat. One of the youngest was trembling. He was a boy Gabriel knew, a friend of his own sons. Gabriel had searched the truck. Now he searched the shed. No, his own sons were not among the men. They had been taken elsewhere. A blessing, Gabriel hoped, because this group seemed to be made up of men labeled Alzados and collaborators. That is what the Instructor had called him, a collaborator.

The young man who was trembling finished his yellow rice with spiced meat and, then, whispering, pressed his palm to Gabriel's shoulder and said, "You're lucky. The noodle soup means they're not going to kill you."

That night, a firefly entered the shed, blinking its eerie greenish light. Hardly any of the men were asleep. They began a whispered debate about the firefly. Was it a signal and, if it was, from God or the devil? Soon there were more fireflies, then a hundred, a thousand, some sort of migration, all flashing in unison the way they did at times, all glowing and appearing to be transformed into tiny living stars.

The men asked each other where could they have taken the women and children. To another shed, nearby, some speculated hopefully. To Trinidad, others assured each other, deposited at the doors of relatives who could care for them while their husbands and fathers were held for questioning.

Halfway through the night the Instructor came into the shed and announced, "Some of you will never again see your families."

In the morning, the men who had eaten yellow rice with spiced meat were taken out and shot against the outside wall of the shed. When the first one was shot, Gabriel heard a weight thudding against the flimsy wall of the shed, and he could smell blood, just the way he smelled it when he slaughtered a pig to be roasted for a guateque.

When all the executions were over, and silence filled the shed, an old man murmured, "Three weeks ago, fifteen soldiers moved into my bohío, so many men in such a small house. My family had to sleep in the barn. The soldiers did nothing all day long, they just sat around eating my crops and my hens, and then one day along came a thousand soldiers, so many that even though they were marching shoulder to shoulder, marching, marching through the cane, like an army of ants, all in a line, but side to side instead of behind each other, even like that, shoulder to shoulder, so many came that you couldn't see where the line of shoulders ended.

"So I went into my house and alerted the fifteen who were loafing there, and one of them said, 'Aah, the cleaning up'."

Now, immobilized in the hospital bed and blinded by darkness, Gabriel recalled the way the old man talked about the limpia, the cleaning up, as if it had not surprised him. "How old are you?" Gabriel had asked, and the old man had answered, "One hundred exactly," and Gabriel had thought to himself, so that's why he's not surprised, because the old man was even older than his own mother, a woman born when the struggles against Spain were just beginning.

The floor of the shed had filled with excrement and urine. After many hours the Instructor came back and took some more men away to be drowned in a tank of water, the kind guajiros used for catching rainwater to quench the thirst of horses. This time everyone had to go outside and watch. Even though Gabriel was grateful for the chance to stretch his legs, he didn't want to watch the drownings, so he turned his head away and watched the horizon instead, blackened cane fields outlined against the sky. When the sounds of the drownings were over, the man who was one hundred years old began sobbing, and when the Instructor told him to shut up, he said, "My son" and Gabriel understood that one of the ones who had been drowned was not really an Alzado, but just the old man's son who had been selected by the Instructor as a likely example for the others.

Again, I got the answering machine. I left another brief cryptic message, trying to imagine the home life of the censor assigned to listen to my call. I wished I had established some sort of code before leaving home, some way of telling my husband about Cuba without sounding like I was criticizing the government, a code like the one Isabelita invented when she wrote to Amparo after my grandmother had emigrated to New York, using the phrase "Gabriel is still working in the garden" when she meant he was still in prison.

I knew that by now my husband would be worried. My children wouldn't understand why I couldn't call them every night the way I would from a trip to any other destination. I swallowed the wave of loneliness and nostalgia, remembering how long I had yearned for Cuba.

I went to the house of Araceli, a cousin so young that I'd never met her before. This time I took the *guagua* since Araceli lived close to the tourist zone and her apartment was not hard to find.

Her entire family greeted me with excitement. As with Miguelito, I was welcomed by embraces and a cascade of questions. Araceli's husband wanted to know all the same things I had answered for Miguelito and the taxi driver, about schools, medical insurance, unemployment, company benefits, the price of cars, salaries.

Araceli ran her palm across the fabric of my dress, saying, "Ay, how pretty, here there is no fabric so pretty. Hardly any fabric at all. Her own dress was worn and faded, even though both her husband and teenage brother were military men with privileges. They wanted to know whether it was true that a *Yanqui* attack was likely to occur any day now, was it true that the island was surrounded by U.S. submarines and battleships preparing for war against Cuba. I knew that by saying no, it wasn't true, I was calling the Maximum Leader a liar.

Araceli's brother asked about the price of athletic shoes and how he could get a visa to travel to the U.S. He was wearing a pair of thongs much too short for his feet.

Travel, I realized, was a euphemism for exile. When young Cubans traveled, they rarely returned. For that reason, the government hardly ever granted young men permission to travel.

I was genuinely surprised. Among military families, I had expected to find abundant privileges and a certain amount of loyalty to the revolution. Araceli's mother said she remembered meeting me briefly in 1960. "That," she added, "was when we still had freedom in Cuba." Then she switched on her black-and-white television to watch the opening of the Pan American games. The entire screen was taken up by a closeup of Fidel's bearded image.

"Ay, Fidelito," she murmured affectionately. I found myself mystified by the contradictions of Fidel's leadership. Even people who felt oppressed by him seemed to regard him with indulgence, the way loving parents continue to love a mischievous child. Or was she mocking him by feigning admiration? Perhaps she was simply in the habit of posturing for visitors from the Neighborhood Committee. I remembered my uncle Juan telling me how he used to have to perform with such caution when he was training for the Olympics trying to strike a balance by playing well enough for the Olympics, but not so well that the Maximum Leader would be humiliated when he came out to practice with the team.

I excused myself and went to the bathroom while Araceli's family watched the opening ceremonies of the Games. In the bathroom there was no running water, just buckets lined up for later use. The path from the living room to the bathroom led down a hall lined with portraits of Fidel and Ché Guevara along with wedding and baby pictures of family members.

When I returned from the bathroom, Araceli's mother apologized for the lack of water and explained that they had to haul it up in buckets from a water truck on the street below. "The pipes are bad. And I have nothing to offer you except water." To illustrate her point she opened the refrigerator and showed me its empty interior.

She said she was angry about the Pan American Games. "All that money," she murmured bitterly, "millions spent building those stadiums and hotels, when we don't have either food or clothes."

Araceli interceded with more questions about the U.S. Like Miguelito, she wanted details. She wanted to understand my daily life, my family, work and surroundings. She seemed bewildered by my choice of a rural home. Hadn't I grown up in the city where everything was very exciting and beautiful?

When I explained that for me the city was like death, her eyes grew wide. I knew she had no basis for imagining the squalor of Spanish Harlem.

"You seem," Araceli said, watching me closely for a response, "to be half-communist. Here, only the very dedicated communists volunteer on farms." Her husband nodded in agreement.

Their appraisal of my rural preference astonished me so much that frowning, I retorted, "Not me! I like freedom of speech! I like to say or write anything I please." In fact, until returning to Cuba I had never thought much about freedom of speech or any other form of freedom. I had never noticed freedom.

Everyone in the room stared at me. "You write?" Araceli asked, crestfallen.

"Just a little poetry," I confessed, but in the back of my mind I kept thinking that soon I would be writing more, speaking to the outside world for Miguelito, for Gabriel.

"Aah," Araceli breathed, astounded. "You mean it's really true that over there anyone at all can write anything they want?"

"Yes."

She looked crushed. "Here," she said softly, "you have to be chosen for a literary course of study and for membership in the Writers Union."

Araceli's mother nudged her elbow. They were sitting close together on the couch, and I could see that her mother wanted her to continue. "She would like to write filmscripts," the older woman said, emphasizing her words by smiling and nodding rapidly.

Araceli nodded also, more slowly. "Yes," she agreed timidly, "I love the Cuban film industry but here it is impossible for me to write."

"Someday perhaps," I offered, wishing I could wrap hope up in packages and offer it to my relatives in place of fragrant soaps and fruit-flavored candies.

I distributed the small gifts, and Araceli's mother seized one of the pens I had tossed into my bag as an afterthought just before leaving the U.S.

"A pen! Look, a pen! I'm going to write a letter!" She sat down alone at the kitchen table. "Pens are very hard to find," she said to me. Then she spent a long time writing, and I went back into the living room with Araceli and her husband and brother to watch the sports event which had suddenly attracted thousands of tourists to Cuba.

"I want you to smuggle this letter to Miami," Araceli's mother told me, tucking an envelope into my open camera bag. "I would like to travel," she added, rolling her eyes in a way Cubans do when they're letting you know they have to be secretive. Her son repeated his hope of traveling also but Araceli took me aside and whispered, "For my mother it is not so difficult, but my brother really shouldn't try to travel because he is a member of the military and he has been accepted into the communist youth group, so for him it could mean big problems."

I had noticed that when Cubans said big problems they were usually referring either to the Neighborhood Committees for the Defense of the Revolution or to the secret police. Cubans knew they could be persecuted or even arrested for expressing a desire to emigrate. Many were sent to forced labor camps in the countryside as punishment for requesting permission to leave the island. For those who did obtain permission, the cost was exorbitant, and had to be paid in dollars, by exiled relatives in the U.S. If the person emigrating had technical or professional skills, the Cuban government demanded reimbursement of the cost of the emigrant's education. Some emigrants were held for years in refugee camps in Central America, while relatives in the U.S. kept trying to come up with enough money to ransom them.

Araceli took me out to a small terrace overlooking the silent, melancholy street. There were no cars or buses in sight, only a few bicycles and pedestrians.

"Could you take me to a dollar store?" Araceli asked timidly. She had suddenly grown very nervous, and her voice was quiet, barely a whisper. The dollar stores were meant for tourists. Cubans were prohibited from entering and they weren't allowed to possess dollars or other foreign currency. Miguelito had warned me that taking Cuban relatives into dollar stores could mean big problems for the Cubans. One of his friends had been interrogated for several hours after entering a dollar store with a relative from the U.S.

"My daughter needs shoes," Araceli explained, embarassed. She knew she was asking me to place her in a dangerous position.

I agreed to take her into one of the hotel shops. Araceli, thrilled, was glowing. She went back into the apartment to awaken her small daughter from a nap. She came back holding the sleepy girl. This time her husband came out onto the terrace as well. They debated the girl's shoe size, and decided they needed an electric fan also. The air was hot and sticky as it always is during the rainy season.

Araceli and I left together, walking toward the tourist zone. As we entered the lobby of one of Cuba's biggest hotels, Araceli's eyes became glazed. She was sweating profusely, and her shoulders were trembling.

"I'm dizzy with fear," she whispered, holding onto my elbow.

"Let's go," I suggested, but she refused, insisting that shoes for her daughter were more important than her apprehension.

A young man in a melon-colored *guayabera* ambled past us, clicking his tongue and shaking his head. Apparently we were not fooling him. "Go on," he said, gesturing toward the shop entrance. We hurried toward the entrance. I glanced around the hotel lobby, reassuring myself that the plainclothesman was really going to let us in. Having to sneak my distant cousin into a store in her own homeland seemed so ludicrous and so unjust that I was left with the feeling that I was a performer in some bizarre surrealistic play.

Inside, we found an eerie assortment of turtle heads mounted on polished boards boasting the single word 'CUBA.' There were also stuffed fledgling ducks and shore birds, wind chimes made of land crabs and moon snails, mounted alligators, flying fish and iguanas. With the economy crumbling, Fidel seemed to have chosen the same route Machado had taken sixty years earlier, the selling off of Cuba's wilderness.

We passed displays of voodoo dolls and figurines of Afro-Cuban deities, racks of embroidered *guayabera* shirts, mountains of straw hats, glass cases featuring famous brands of Cuban cigars and rum. Finally, we found a room filled with shoes of every style and size. Araceli deliberated for a long agonizing moment. She had never been faced with abundance, and the chance to choose confused her. Finally she settled on a pair of tiny yellow canvas slip-ons.

"Comrade," Araceli called to the Cuban salesgirl, a government employee like everyone else in the tourist industry. I cringed, wishing I had warned my cousin that foreigners didn't address people as 'Comrade'. The salesgirl glared at us indulgently. I paid with dollars, showing my U.S. passport as identification. The plainclothes guard turned away as we continued moving through the store until we found a case displaying electric fans.

Araceli had relaxed by now. When we emerged onto the street with her packages in our arms, she leaned toward me, pressing her shoulder against mine and whispered, "Now I see that I'm not the first Cuban to enter one of those stores!" The ban against shopping in dollar stores seemed to be as unpredictable as the black market. In Cuba, breaking the rules could mean big problems for known dissidents, and official indifference for everyone else. The constant fear came from worrying about your neighbors' perceptions of your dedication to Fidel.

As we walked toward one of the yellow and red *guagua* buses, I stepped over a bundle of brown paper someone had dropped on the sidewalk. Looking down, I noticed the beak of a chicken protruding from one end of the package.

"*Santería*," Araceli whispered. Someone is placing a curse on the tourists.

"We are afraid," she said a moment later and, not knowing whether she was referring to the voodoo-style curse, the secret police, the failing Cuban economy or the tense political situation, I just nodded and we kept walking. "Yes," Araceli repeated, "we are very afraid."

I spent one last afternoon with Miguelito, listening to his songs about love and fear. I stayed later than I had planned and by the time I departed, I could think of no words to leave behind as floating buoys in the sea which seemed to surround my cousin's isolation. Hearing him confine his music, once again, to the darkness of that room, I experienced a resurgence of dismay, wondering whether he, like the small irridescent *totí* bird which had crashed into the glass wall of a seaside restaurant, would be rinsed off and set outdoors, revived.

Aurora embraced me quietly, with tears. Miguelito said, "Well, I know that it could be a very long time until we see each other again." A thousand possibilities surged across my lips, but the only words I could come up with were, "Write to me."

───── ⚬⁄⚬ ─────

On the afternoon of his release from the punishment cell, Gabriel's eyes began to throb as the light seeped into them. Never once in all his life of nearly sixty years had he imagined that darkness could be so terrifying. He felt like a child afraid of the small sounds of nature, the songs of tree frogs, the squeals of wild pigs, sounds heard all day without inducing fear, sounds which became visible at night, taking on monstrous images. In the punishment cell, darkness had become unlike any other horror Gabriel had ever known, not a void but paralysis in the midst of great activity, invisible, swarming activity. The cell had become a forest where even the sound of movement within his bloodstream pounded in Gabriel's ears.

The Instructor passed along an aisle between two rows of hospital cots and, glancing in Gabriel's direction, announced, "Sixty-three days in the punishment cell, eh, guajiro, was it enough?" The Instructor halted at the foot of Gabriel's cot, and even though Gabriel couldn't see his form, the voice was unmistakable. It was the same voice he had half-listened to during every interrogation, a chopped, enraged voice made more furious by Gabriel's inability to listen with both ears. No matter how hard he'd tried to believe that the interrogations were real, only half of his being obeyed while the other half clung to its disbelief, regarding the Instructor from a great distance, seeing a mouth opening and closing, but refusing to accept the stream of words.

Now Gabriel made a movement, trying to sit up in the hospital cot. He realized he was immobile, paralyzed or tied. He let himself drift away from the Instructor's familiar voice, expecting to feel the blow of a rifle or fist against his eyes.

"First a little light, some soup, then some exercise," the Instructor was saying, "and after you enter the rehabilitation program, you can start having visitors from time to time, your wife, daughters, sisters. . ."

Gabriel knew his mouth wouldn't work even if he had anything to say that hadn't already been repeated a thousand times. "I did nothing." How many times had he actually repeated the single word 'nothing', by itself, as if it could explain itself for him, take his place in the impossibly dark cell. How many times had the Instructor agreed that there were no charges, just questions.

Right before they put him into the punishment cell, Gabriel had finally shrieked, out of exasperation, "Unless you tell me where my family is, you'll get nothing from me!" Only that time the word 'nothing' came out wrong, sounding like a veil for something obscured, convincing the Instructor that Gabriel might be one of those guajiros who actually did know something about the locations of Alzado hideouts.

"We know how you guajiros," the Instructor had said quietly, clenching his teeth with outrage, "are all connected, each family tangled up with all the others, brothers and cousins and nephews spread out all over the countryside, everyone married to his neighbor's sister or niece, a pot of beans always waiting for whomever comes along the road.

"Mamonsillo," the Instructor had said, "mamonsillo", repeating the name of the fruit as if its sound could make everything clear to Gabriel. "That's what we found in the stomachs of three bandits we shot in the mountains a couple of months ago. You did have mamonsillo trees on your land?"

Gabriel had grasped only the emphasized word 'did', only the past tense of the word with its threat that the farm might no longer belong to him.

"I do," Gabriel had answered. "I do have a mamonsillo grove, but it's wild fruit, planted by God."

That was when they took the light away. When he recovered from the beating and found himself enclosed within the blackness of the punishment cell, he began to stir, measuring the cell with paces, two paces by three, with a hole in the floor at one end. The door of the cell was covered with sheet metal, hot in the afternoon and cold at night.

They brought in another man, a stranger, and the two of them faced each other in darkness, wondering how they could both sleep in the narrow space without touching the foul stench around the hole in the floor. The man turned out to be a priest from Havana. He ripped up his shirt and began writing scriptures all over the cloth of one sleeve, using blood instead of ink. Gabriel could hear the invisible actions, and he asked the man to explain what he was doing.

"Ezekiel," the man said, "on my shirt, with blood, because I have no ink. Wounds and words are the only things one owns in prison, no? You can write them in the dark, by feel. 'The Lord God says: You are so proud you think you are God, sitting on the throne of a god on your island home in the midst of the seas.'

"For those words of Ezekiel, I was arrested. So now I write the words again and, so, defy him."

Gabriel could hear the man's voice, but he could see nothing. The man continued.

"'Therefore I brought forth fire from your own actions and let it burn you to ashes upon the earth in the sight of all those watching you.'"

The man paused, then said, "I wrote those words on a wall in Havana, on the day when he first called himself Maximum Leader. Imagine the arrogance, the pride?"

Gabriel tried to listen, but he couldn't stop thinking about his wife and family, his land. "They poisoned the well," Gabriel said into the darkness. "They slaughtered every last animal, all the cows and horses, the bull, carcasses spread out over the land, left there for the vultures to eat. You never saw so many black wings flapping down out of the sky! I did nothing. I fed no one. They say I fed my cousins who were fighting, but I fed no one, how could I? For weeks there had been no visitors, not with the roads blocked and all the talk of danger. Of course I had fed his troops before, the Barbudos, cousins and strangers too, because I did really believe they were going to bring us justice and freedom, elections and..."

Then the darkness sliced itself open, and someone moved into the cell to take the priest away. Gabriel stayed alone in the cell for a month, without bathing, then another month, and when he finally asked what had happened to his cellmate, the Instructor said , "El paredón, the firing wall. He was only shot with blanks, to scare him, but even so, he died. For most people, blanks are enough. Fear, more powerful than death itself, eh?"

That day, when Gabriel's dinner of chickpeas came, he left it untouched. His eyes had finally adjusted to the darkness, and he could vaguely discern the movements of maggots in the bowl of garbanzos. The worms were dead, boiled along with the food, but they came floating up to the surface, twisting and pale.

———∿———

Since childhood I'd known about my great-uncle Gabriel's arrest. I remembered it as something which had been frozen in time, something which never changed. Abuelita Amparo received letters from her sister Isabelita in Trinidad, and the letters always ended with the code phrase, "Gabriel is still in the garden." Like most northerners, I had grown up with the illusion that everyone in prison had been tried and convicted, proven guilty beyond any reasonable doubt. Yet I knew Gabriel loved only his land and his work. I knew he was neither cruel nor selfish, and that if he had a weakness, it was only his fierce dedication to the land. When I thought of Gabriel, I saw him on a horse, cantering and shaking his fist at the devil.

During years of nostalgia, the one possibility I had never considered was the grim truth, that along with Gabriel, his entire family had been imprisoned and that now, three decades later, they were still held captive, and that along with those who had been alive when the farm was swallowed by the Maximum Leader, even the newborn babies were being born into permanent captivity.

———∿———

On the afternoon of his release from the punishment cell, Gabriel discovered that his mouth was regaining its movement, and that as his eyesight gradually returned, he could make out the shape of the Instructor's head, a blurry outline far away from him, at the foot of the bed, a distance of galaxies.

"Yes," he finally sighed, responding to the Instructor's repeated command. "Yes," he said, thinking of his wife and his children and their children, remembering the surprise on little Taíno's face as his body was hurled across the boundary separating earth and sky. "If it means I can have visitors, then yes, I will accept your rehabilitation program. Yes, I will enter the training program and learn to weave baskets for the tourist industry and for export."

"Good," the Instructor's voice seemed to come floating across space, fading into the sky behind his blurry head. Gabriel reached for the papers, startled by the movement of his own hand. He signed them without reading, knowing that the words no longer mattered. When his meal of maggot-infested noodles arrived, Gabriel refused to eat the pale, twisting forms. "No," his voice floated toward the orderly, "my best pig is roasting in the ground, and today I am going to eat it with a sauce of wild honey and sour oranges."

Dreaming again, he lifted first one wing, then the other, and away he soared, rising high above the prisonyard, glancing down at his hospital cot, at the assortment of angular buildings, at the punishment wing called Boniatico, with its black, metallic cells, thinking, as he flew, that Little Sweet Potato was a very soft name for such a rugged place, and that never again in his life, if he lived, would he be able to taste his favorite coconut and sweet potato pudding without feeling the touch of blood in his eyes.

When Gabriel awakened from his flight, a man in the next bed was talking to him. Gabriel looked across the expanse between cots and saw that the other man was flying too, without wings, flat on his back on the gray cot, peering over the edge, gazing down at the sea far below, the sea where each wave had its myriad tiny almond-shaped glints of light resembling so many eyes.

"Once," Gabriel said to the man in the next bed, "when I was very young and my brother was studying history, I asked him about the sea, about the way it sometimes looks like it's filled with eyes, and he answered me with something about physics and refraction, and then he said that there was a time when Spanish slave ships kept people in cloth sacks in case they got caught by the British, who had prohibited the running of Africans to the islands. And when a Spanish captain thought he was about to be caught by a British patrol, he just tossed the sacks into the ocean, saying they were sacks of coal, and then he headed back to the Congo for more.

"My mother," Gabriel added, drifting from sea to land, was married twice, once in a guava thicket, and later in church."

Gabriel went on to tell the whole story of his mother's two weddings, the first a make-believe ceremony enacted by a child.

"She wore a tail of banana leaf," Gabriel murmured, his eyes wandering through the guava thicket, searching for ghosts. "Along came a grown man from town and he saw this little fifteen-year-old guajirita dressed in a shiny green wedding dress made of leaves, and he liked her, so he tried to talk to her, but she ran away and hid under the guava trees, because she was just a child and strangers frightened her, and at fifteen she knew much more about cattle than she did about men, because she had always lived on the farm and to her it was the only place that ever seemed really safe. To me too.

"So this gentleman from town saw her and liked her, and he went to her father's house and asked for her hand in marriage and, of course, her father agreed, because the stranger looked respectable and, in fact, he was an educated man who knew more about town than he did about the land.

"But my mother wasn't a woman who would leave the land easily. She kept her husband on the farm through thirteen births, and then, when he left her to travel to faraway places, South America, I think, and he came back sick and died young, leaving her with all those children, still she wouldn't move into town. Not until she was very old did she move into town to live with my sister. You never saw anyone who clung to the land like that old woman. She's still alive now, in Trinidad, and you can imagine how it will affect her when she learns that the well was poisoned and that they slaughtered not only the cattle, but even the horses.

"My parents started that herd from a single mare and stallion. Like Noah."

The sky went dark, and Gabriel's memory floated back into the punishment cell, the black cubicle which reminded him of caves and tunnels. He remembered the stories his half-yanqui niece had told him about whole trains moving underground, like worms in the earth, full of living people whose eyes have grown accustomed to dull colors and dim light, to brown sky and...

"The slaves of Cobre fought for two centuries before they finally convinced the Spaniards to let them be free. And that was nearly a hundred years before any of the other slaves were freed."

Gabriel heard his own voice from a great distance. He was underwater now and all around him there were eyes and fish, mermaids and turtles.

"Dead people can't fly," he said. "My aunt was the daughter of a Congolese slave and she told me that only the living can fly. Dead people don't need to fly. Once there was a plantation where so many slaves flew away all at once that the whole sugar mill had to close down. Put them out of business."

Gabriel felt a deep, wrenching pain inside his bones. "That floor has ruined me," he moaned. "And to think, once I wanted nothing more than a stone floor!" He pushed himself up out of the water, and looked down into the face of the hundred-year-old man whose son had been drowned as an example set by reptile-green soldiers.

"In heaven," Gabriel whispered to the corpse, "there will be horses."

———⌀———

Gasoline was so scarce that I decided to travel like a Cuban, giving up great volumes of time instead of paying the thousand dollars *Cubatur* was demanding for a car rental to Trinidad and back. On the first bus I leafed through travel brochures advertising Pinar del Río, the province where Gabriel's family had been held captive for three decades. The brochures featured glossy colored photographs of campgrounds, hunting reserves, bass lakes and limestone caverns, including the caves where Cuban troops were headquartered during the Missile Crisis of 1962. Shiny waterfalls, rustic baskets replete with mounds of exotic tropical fruit, cheerful *guajiros* plucking tobacco leaves and chopping sugarcane, dignified gentlemen rolling cigars. 'Some of the best tobacco in the world,' I read, 'is cultivated in the municipality of Sandino.' And I imagined Gabriel's grandchildren working there, in the tobacco fields surrounding their captive town, on the tail of the alligator, waiting.

On the second bus I flipped through more brochures, finding Trinidad with its medieval stone houses clustered along cobblestone streets.

Looking up from the brochures, I gazed out the bus window at field after field of towering green sugarcane and row after row of work-camp barracks, village after silent village, groups of people waiting without speaking to each other.

As a child I had measured the entire world against Cuba. But it was a magical Cuba, an imagined Cuba. It was not this forbidding landscape of soldiers and modernized barracoons.

Turning back to the brochures, I read about *la provincia de Sancti Spiritus*, the province of the Holy Spirit, and about the founding of *La Villa de la*

Santísima Trinidad, the Town of the Holy Trinity, in 1514. I scanned glossy images of the town square, churches, and palaces converted to museums, and beyond, the Escambray Mountains. In one picture an old man walked a caged bird, much the way people in other countries walk their pet dogs.

———∽———

On the afternoon of Gabriel's release from the punishment cell, two orderlies removed the centenarian's corpse from the cot next to Gabriel's and dumped, in its place, a young Alzado wounded in both legs.

"Out of each group that they catch," the youth told Gabriel dreamily, "they may decide to leave one or two alive, trying to prove that they take prisoners. In case the foreign press ever gets around to covering this war. The way they covered his war. I was with him, you know? I still keep the beard, because I was proud to be with him in the Sierra Maestra. But then when he changed...or maybe he didn't change at all, maybe we just didn't see him clearly...

"Now," the boy's voice faded, "I don't expect to see my family again."

He turned toward Gabriel and asked, "If you live through this, will you tell someone about me, so he can tell someone else and so on, until someone finds my mother and explains it all to her?"

Gabriel agreed. "This morning," he said, "I was blind and dying, then I survived, but I was lost, first in the sky, then in the sea. Finally, here I am again, back to earth, but now, if God wills, I might live a very long time yet, whether I want to or not."

So the boy told Gabriel all about the first war, about hiding in the mountains and coming out victorious, carried along by the people's cheers, a hero.

"I rode into Havana on the back of a flatbed truck, on the day Batista fled, and such a crowd greeted us, people lining all the streets on both sides, people standing along every inch of the sea wall, cheering, laughing, singing, the flags rippled by wind, so many flags that you can't imagine the red triangles, the blue and white stripes.

"I had lost three brothers in the fighting and my father, two uncles, seven cousins, four nephews. The women were dancing, kissing us, reaching up onto the trucks to touch our beards and our hands, laughing, after so much war, everyone laughing again and dancing. The sea wall, on one side, was holding back the ocean and the sky, and on the other side it was holding in a flood of happiness like nothing you've ever seen, so many people celebrating, so much happiness, and how long we'd waited to be happy!

"So at first they put us to work just guarding everything while Fidel was trying to clean up the mess left behind by the war and then, next thing you know, I hear that one of my distant cousins has been shot in the moat of El Morro Castle, without a trial, just shot, and this cousin was like me, someone who had fought for Fidel, not against him, so I started to wonder what was wrong and then, when they kept shooting people who had done nothing and when I saw the crowds shouting "Al paredón, al paredón," everyone wanting to send someone else to the firing wall, then I walked away from Havana and hitched a ride back to Cienfuegos where I was born, and I'd left Havana without thinking, without planning, leaving everything behind, and when I got to Cienfuegos I walked into my house and it was my nineteenth birthday, and I kissed my mother and took my grandfather's hunting rifle and all the ammunition I could find, and a piece of cloth to use as a blanket, and I walked all the way to Escambray and climbed up into the mountains and along the way I ran into others who were doing the same thing, who were angry because they'd learned about someone who'd been shot for no reason, or because they'd heard that he was going to take our land and there would be no more stores, no street vendors, and everyone wanted to know, how are we going to make a living if we can't buy or sell? And then when I was up there, in the mountains, and I had a lot of time to spend thinking about what had happened, I realized that we hadn't just been happy after all, we'd been delirious, all of us in the streets of Havana that day, soldiers and children and old women and prostitutes, delirious, the way you get after a fever."

When the boy fell silent, Gabriel asked the question which had been disturbing him. "How many Alzados are up there in the Escambray?"

And the boy's answer disturbed him even more than the nagging question.

"Scattered groups, five men here, ten there, twenty in another, perhaps a few hundred total, or maybe a thousand, two thousand altogether, not much more, spread across the entire mountain range."

Gabriel felt himself floating again, the cot a raft on a hot sea, the water streaked green and blue, filled with the eyes of drowned slaves. Then he was underwater, strange creatures peering out at him from crevices in a reef of pink and orange coral, a reef the color of flamingos at sunset.

Later, he surfaced and heard the boy still murmuring, and he wondered, once again, how there could have been such a war brewing in the mountains so close to his farm, and how he could have been so oblivious, so convinced that the last battle had ended when Fidel marched into Havana with his truckloads of Barbudos.

Gabriel heard the mooing of a cow and he scanned the horizon, counting his herd, feeling the rolling canter of his stallion. He turned toward the boy in the next cot and said, "Soon the rains will end."

Then he asked the boy to tell him what it was like in the mountains, and the boy explained that it was just like the pictures of the inferno he'd seen as a child when he sneaked into his father's library and leafed through old art books from Spain.

"Did you ever see those pictures the Spanish priests painted to show how the Indians were burned at the stake?" The boy spoke with his eyes closed, and Gabriel could tell by his voice that he was in pain.

"I saw the pictures," Gabriel answered, "and now I hear the screams." Then he told the boy how Daniel's tales had always brought him nightmares, because it was too hard to understand how men could have survived the terrors of being lost at sea and then, when they arrived, turned their energies toward setting other men on fire. Gabriel remembered lying awake thinking that maybe God, having such a big world to keep track of, sometimes forgot about little places like Cuba.

"So much sugar in Cuba," Gabriel told the boy, reciting an old folk saying, "and here we are still drinking our coffee bitter."

Then the boy told him how Fidel's troops had found him.

"We knew they were coming. From up there you could see them approaching, marching shoulder to shoulder across the flat lands, forming a ring around us. We were surrounded. I climbed a palm and hid up there in the top of the tree, right below the fronds, where I could see everything. The troops had to scatter, as they came up the side of the mountain, because there was too much vegetation for them to stay in their straight lines.

"We were ten, and they were a thousand or more. No, not ten, only seven, because two had already been lost to fever the week before, and one had been wounded and had to stay behind in a cave.

"So along they came like that, firing mortars and machine guns, a big ragged circle closing in, and if it had been at night maybe we could have broken through the line but not in daylight. It would have been suicide, so I stayed up there in the tree, hoping they would pass below without spotting me, because they were firing low, expecting us to be crouched under bushes or in the ditches we dug for hiding whenever we couldn't find a cave.

"I had an M52 and my machete, both from a militiaman I'd ambushed down near a cane field. I watched them coming along, and we were all up in the trees, looking down at them from our grove of palms, coffee farms up above, and the forest, and sugar below, and the river, and some ponds. At night I had gotten used to drinking out of the ponds on the farms below but sometimes if we were too high in the mountains to go down to the ponds and, if we were too far from a stream and if it rained, I would drink the water that got trapped in holes in the rocks. I carried a hollow reed with me to use as a straw for drinking out of rocks. And there were bees nesting among the rocks, so we always had wild honey, and I kept a few pieces of limes and sugarcane in my knapsack to suck on when I was hungry. When we killed a jutía we ate the meat soaked in lime juice because, unless we were down in a cave, it was too dangerous to build a fire and risk being spotted by the smoke, so we soaked the meat with lime juice and covered it over with yagruma leaves and spread it out on the rocks to be cooked by the sun.

"We always came up with something to eat, wild game or gifts of food from the guajiros because yes, it's true, they helped us a lot and they gave us medicines too, the medicines they used on their horses, and they knew how to make plasters of tobacco and herbs. Sometimes they gave us the ammunition from their hunting rifles, and that's why you're here because he knew what he was doing, clearing out all the guajiros to keep them from helping us, and that's why it's all been kept so secret, because what would people think if they learned that the peasants are opposing his plan? How would it make him look if people knew that even the poorest farmers didn't want to give away their shacks and their fields, their dreams of crops?

"I had a lot of sores on my legs from the ticks, but whenever we got to a good cave and could make a good fire, I burned the sores clean with the flat of my machete heated in the flames.

"With the limpia, they thought they had cleaned us up but others are still up there, and even when they catch the last Alzado and slice open his stomach to see what he's been eating so they can try to guess which guajiros have been feeding him, even then we'll be like new cicadas, waiting beneath the soil until we can crawl out into the sun someday, singing. When a cicada finally gets loose, you know, there's no shutting it up.

"It was impossible to stay clean up there. For me, that was the worst of all. I brushed my teeth with crushed mango leaves, thinking that with such a smell of turpentine, the leaves must be good for cleaning."

The boy fell silent. Gabriel wanted to know how it had ended. Had the olive green line of men passed beneath the palm trees without seeing the hidden Alzados? Had one of the soldiers suddenly glanced up to see a foot clinging to the gray trunk of a palm? Or maybe one of the seven Alzados had spooked, like a new horse, firing down from his tree, alarming the snaking line of troops below.

To ask struck Gabriel as irreverent. Perhaps the boy would never tell anyone how the day of his defeat had ended. Perhaps, thought Gabriel, feeling his body float along the surface of the cot, no one would ever tell the boy's mother how he had fought from the top of a tree, and been captured. Suddenly Gabriel began to wonder whether anyone would ever learn the story of his own capture, of his wife, his sons and daughters, the grandchildren, little Taíno soaring through the air, looking more surprised than afraid.

"If I survive to climb out into that sun, singing, like your insect friend, then," Gabriel sighed, "I will tell the whole thing bit by bit, in every detail, as well as I can remember and, someday, a century from now when people hear the tale, they'll be no more inclined to believe it than we are when we hear about the Indians or the slaves." But maybe God will be glad to hear us still talking after we are dead. Gabriel's last thought drifted into the streaked water, entwined by strands of translucent seaweed. He thought of the legend of the Virgin of Cobre descending from the sky during a storm to rescue three fishermen who were about to drown because they'd filled their boat so full of salt that it was sinking from the weight.

He told the boy about his cousins Omar, Emilio and Adán, and their brother Alvaro who was still with Fidel's troops. "Only the triumph is gone now," Gabriel added, "used up. It comes in very small packets, and once it is gone, then you need another war or maybe a chance to find some other kind of triumph..." His voice trailed away across the sea.

He heard the boy saying yes, he knew Emilio and Adán for sure, Alzados, yes, fighting with guns stolen from their brother Alvaro. Omar, maybe, but it was hard to tell with so many men in the mountains, and Omar was a common enough name.

"Funny isn't it," the boy was saying, "how those guajira women like to pick out pretty names for their sons from stories they've heard or poems someone read in a schoolbook. Even the women who never went to school know how to choose the most exotic names. In the mountains I met so many kids called Adonis, Demetrio and Orestes that I couldn't keep them all straight. I kept expecting to see horses with wings, centaurs, dragons, satyrs, nymphs. Can you read, old man?"

"Read?" Gabriel caught the image of the phrase 'old man' and held it, staring at the face that must have been his own, the body made crooked by the punishment cell floor, the hair falling out from lack of fresh fruit, the skin fading from polished mahogany to stone-cracked wheat. He could see a hand pounding the wheat, grasping a gray oval grinding stone, raising it up into the air, bringing it down against the dry grain, crushing it against a concave surface of stone, preparing a meal of human flesh.

"Eh, can you, if you can't it's okay, I can teach you."

"Read? Yes, I know how to read. I went to school, plenty of school. You don't know my mother. She wouldn't have allowed me to take over the farm unless I'd finished school, and not just primary, either, a technical course, animal husbandry. Living in town to go to school was miserable though, for me, the way I am, no space, no time.

"There's not a sugar mill on this island that could make my mother sell her land, my land, not even if we were starving. They tried." So much money they offered her for those caballerías of good soil, but never would she sell, never, and he was just like his mother, he wouldn't give up the land just by accepting rehabilitation. It would always be there, until God decided to roll up the world and put it away, until that last day, there would be land.

"Your women," the boy said, "do you know what happened to them?"

Gabriel shook his head, feeling pain surge across his chest and shoulders, searing the skin of his neck, chewing on his eyes.

"Everyone says they've been taken to Miramar," the boy volunteered, "the women and children of El Escambray and the farms below, from Cienfuegos to Trinidad, imagine! That's a lot of farms, thousands, tens of thousands! They say a lot of the women and children are being held prisoner in the mansions of Miramar." The boy soldier watched Gabriel's transformed face as the old man heard these words.

Miramar! Look at the sea! The mansions abandoned by the wealthy when they realized that Fidel was going to take away their land and money. Miramar. What would his wife do, trapped inside the four walls of a mansion? And yet, it meant they were alive, trapped, but breathing, waiting.

I realized that I had been a visitor on my great-uncle's farm only a few months before Gabriel and his entire family were taken away. Now, more than ever, I felt like a spectator watching a science fiction movie, recognizing relatives on the screen.

At best, his reign would end swiftly, bypassing the waterfall of blood predicted by Miguelito. At worst, it would drag on indefinitely. And what about Miguelito? He might at some point drop his guard, become an overt, outspoken dissident and end up in prison. Miguelito was sane, but they could send him to a psychiatric ward where men fought over food and set each other's socks on fire while they were sleeping.

Perhaps Miguelito would receive no diagnosis, only a long punishment like Nicolás Guillén Landrián, the nephew of Cuba's late poet laureate Nicolás Guillén, famous for his poems bemoaning the fate of Cuba's poor. The great poet's nephew was a filmmaker. In 1973 the authorities that censor films discovered that a scene in his documentary, *Coffea Arabica*, showed the Maximum Leader climbing a mountain while a Beatles' song, 'Fool on the Hill,' played in the background.

Miguelito's songs might be reviewed. The words could be analyzed. A problem might be discerned. Offensive verses would be dismantled. Miguelito could find himself trapped inside a place where the sane quickly lost their sanity. I wondered about Gabriel and his years in prison, whether he had snapped or managed to cling to a vine of hope.

Nicolás Guillén Landrián

———— ⌒ ————

On the evening of his release from prison, Gabriel struggled to con-
centrate his mind on the creation of invisible foods. Scanning his memory for everything he had ever eaten, he chose the best to keep him sane
while he waited to see if this time it was really true that he would be
moved to the tail of the alligator to join his family, his resettled family.
Resettled. It was the Instructor's term. The Instructor told tales of a
fine new modern city and no one believed him, not even Gabriel, who
had fallen for the Instructor's promises repeatedly, the promised visits,
the promised delivery of letters from home, the new home, the fine,
modern-city home and the promises of freedom.

The Instructor's words never seemed to mean what they should have
meant. Gabriel always came away feeling like a hungry man who had
been dreaming about food and had awakened to find his belly still empty.

Gabriel had developed a talent for imagining food. He could
describe food in such a way that his cellmates ended up craving generous guajiro dishes. At first it had started as a game, each man telling the
others about something he'd eaten in the outside world, where food
without maggots still existed.

Gabriel started with fruit trees and living animals, cattle, pigs, chickens. He would describe the height of the tree, the color and sheen of a
leaf, the texture of bark, shape of a fruit, acidity of the soft flesh, size and
number of seeds. He composed a verbal textbook of animal husbandry for
the entertainment of his cellmates, delineating every detail of the livestock from their smells to the imprints of their hoofs in the soil, ending
with the way they tasted when served in a sauce of garlic and spice.

By the end of his third year in prison, Gabriel had been nicknamed
the Chef for his descriptions of duck stuffed with pineapple, sea turtle
stewed in its own shell, flying fish draped with avocado sauce and
almonds. His words could make the men taste manioc bread filled with
spiced beef. In Gabriel's presence the men could imagine themselves
consuming mountains of "Moors and Christians," black beans served
with white rice. Land crabs steamed with coconut milk, guava paste
sliced with cheese, marañón jelly from the heart-shaped red fruit of the
cashew tree. Milk whipped with orange mamey fruit, fritters of ñame

tubers, twice-fried ripe plantains. Boniatillo, to make the men laugh. Sweet potato pudding simmered with cream and coconut. The name of the pudding sounded so much like Boniatico, the punishment wing, that each man swore he would never eat sweet potato unless it was served in some other language.

Sweetened corn meal with anise and cinnamon. Burnt-milk candy.

Three years. In three years they had taught him to be satisfied with the illusion of food. They'd stripped him down to bare spirit, with only the hope of eating. He'd mastered the basketweaving. He'd learned to love the smell of a finished basket, the smell of palm leaf and dry reed. His hands, once as hard and dark as wood, were now pliable, like the strips of softened reed, faded like the dry palm leaves, pale, he thought, like maggots. Three years and now he might see for himself how his family had survived, whether the lines on his wife's face had changed, whether his sons had managed to protect the grandchildren from their sudden fright. A person could die of fright. A person could grow ill from sadness. Some diseases were like ghosts. No one could find them, yet they breathed a cold terror to let you know they were there. These were diseases of the soul.

A chicken stuffed with red bananas and rum.

Gabriel's daily fantasies of food always gave way to his attempts at reconstructing the loss of the farm, and the vision of his wife enclosed inside the walls of a Havana mansion. He imagined her gazing out, looking at the sea, looking away from the island. He imagined her forgetting him, believing them if they told her he was dead, lost forever. Because they would tell her things like that. They liked to play tricks on people. One day they would tell you that your family was dead. The next day they would say it was all a joke. That way you never knew what to believe, so you believed nothing.

Like Alvaro. One day, when Gabriel had been inside the prison walls for nearly two years, the Instructor came along and abruptly changed his duty from basketweaving to removal of half-dead men from the punishment cells. The Instructor himself accompanied Gabriel from cell to cell, and Gabriel, following the Instructor's instructions, rolled limp bodies out of the hot dark cubicles, reaching into the darkness, tugging at hands and feet.

Finally they came to a man who was barely alive, with maggots burrowing in the flesh of his scalp, and Gabriel recognized his cousin

Alvaro. The rotting flesh stank. Gabriel drew back, horrified. The Instructor watched him. Then he was led away for another interrogation, even though he knew nothing about his cousin's battles in the mountains, about the day of changing from one of Fidel's officers to one of his enemies. Alvaro, like his brothers, must have decided to take up arms against the Maximum Leader but how could he, Gabriel, on his farm or in this prison, have known about that? Gabriel left the interrogation feeling that more than his flesh had been beaten, feeling that somehow he had betrayed his cousin just by recognizing him in such a defeated form.

Later, when Alvaro miraculously recovered from his months in the punishment cell, with new flesh and new hair, the two cousins encountered each other in a cage-like exercise yard, and Alvaro told Gabriel that his mother had died in Trinidad without finding out that the farm had been confiscated. Gabriel heard the words with immense relief. She had been too old for such sorrow. The joy of knowing she had been kept ignorant surpassed the shock at news of her death. Gabriel kept thinking that if only he had been allowed to visit her on her death-bed, he could have described for her the health of the cattle, the height of the cane. He could have helped keep the secret of its loss.

Gabriel had looked into his cousin's eyes, there in the small enclosed yard, while Alvaro explained that Isabelita had kept her mother ignorant by buying produce on the black market and telling her that it came from the farm and had been sent by Gabriel.

Gabriel remembered the day years ago when news reached the farm that Alvaro had been arrested by Batista's secret police for something he said while playing dominoes, while a neighbor put one ear to the wall and heard the name Fidel. Gabriel, looking at Alvaro in the exercise yard, was now baffled by the trick that years had played on his cousin, sending him first to prison for siding with Fidel and, later, for siding against Fidel. Either way, it seemed like Fidel had taken over the insides of the man, just as the maggots had taken over his flesh. Either way, Fidel seemed to have consumed everyone in Cuba. Gabriel visualized Fidel as an enormous mouth, opening and closing, sending out words and swallowing people.

Then Alvaro had gone on, whispering in the exercise yard while they walked side by side, two men trapped in a big cage.

"They shot Emilio in the mountains," Alvaro whispered, "and

Adán in Trinidad, right there in the town square for everyone to see, right there in front of the church where everyone who passed was sure to see his body and take it as a warning. Now I am in here, and only Omar is still free. The second limpia took away every last guajiro family. No one remains. Now, if Omar goes up into the mountains, it will be suicide. So I pray that he stays below, and finds some other way, some way of pretending to be with him even though he can't possibly be, not now, not after seeing the body of Adán left like that in the plaza, with vultures landing on it, for all the children of Trinidad to see.

Cheese drowned in mango sauce. Gabriel, back in his cell, had pulled his mind away from the plight of his cousins. Dried beef soaked in Spanish sherry. Deep-fried eggs with rice.

He opened his eyes, hearing the resounding alarm. Men were running in all directions, shouting, "Search!" Gabriel sighed. One more search, perhaps, for him soon to be freed, the last. Men were scurrying to hide their cigarettes, letters and poems. The cell door opened, and Gabriel saw the gleaming flat of the guard's machete as the metal descended to send him into darkness, tasting blood.

Field after field of sugarcane passed beyond the bus window. My thoughts fell back to the human rights bulletins, to a sailor denounced by his own brothers for exchanging foreign currency. After being held for seven months in Mazorra, the Psychiatric Hospital, the sailor was transferred to prison. After his release, he was arrested again for trying to leave the country. Later he was arrested for distributing dissident literature and, again for attempting to seek asylum at the Ecuadorian embassy. I thought of his repeated sentences to psychiatric wards, and of the 24 electric shock treatments, and the psychotropic drugs he was forced to take, and of the way he lost his memory and how, at first, he couldn't recognize his wife when it was all over. I thought of all the strangers listed in the human rights bulletins. And I thought of Gabriel, who by living in prison while I was free in the North, had also become a stranger.

On the evening of his release from the forced labor camp, Gabriel began to circle the rows of barracks which, for nearly twenty-seven years now, he had silently called barracones in his mind, the slave barracoons of plantation days. Gabriel had been thinking of himself as a slave since the day of his release from prison, when he found that by release they meant transfer. Now, after three years in prison and nearly twenty-seven years in the labor camp, Gabriel realized that for him, release would come only with death. Even today, when they were finally letting him leave the fenced and guarded camp forever, it was only because he was too old to work and, with his eyesight failing, his baskets were no longer fit for the admiration of tourists. They tried to make him weave straw hats, but his fingers were frozen by arthritis, and his vision had been blurry ever since the last search at Boniato, when a guard opened the cell door and hit him in the face with the flat of a machete, one last blow, intended as a warning, a reminder that he could be sent back to the punishment cells whenever they decided he was leaning toward rebellion.

They poisoned the well. Gabriel had taken to remembering how they poisoned the well and slaughtered the milk cows, the red colt, the fighting cocks. After Boniato he gave up imagining food, and set his mind to remembering instead, living over and over, through dark and light, the morning when he came back from a stroll to the river and found his house burning, the horses and cattle bleeding, and little Taíno flying through the sky into a truck, full of grandchildren.

Gabriel had even become a collector of other people's memories. He kept them deep inside himself, along with his own past, gathered from the stories told by other guajiros in the labor camp, and by the captured Alzados at Boniato, Alvaro and all the others.

The last alzado had been killed in the Sierra de Escambray decades ago, in 1966. No one dared to rise up in arms anymore. Everyone agreed it would be suicide. Martyrdom and suicide were as different as soil and dirt. Suicides always took others down along with them. Martyrs inspired others to lift themselves up, to face the sky with its turbulent clouds and singing angels.

Occasionally they let Gabriel leave the penal camp for a weekend furlough to visit his wife in the nearby Captive Town. The town had turned out to be neither fine nor modern and, in Gabriel's mind it wasn't a real town but an extension of the prison camps, a camp without fences–the illusion of a town. Gabriel's family couldn't leave without permission, and his grandchildren and great-grandhildren were just as much captives as his wife. Even the children born long after the sweeping up of El Escambray, even they were captives, held under a life sentence which was much more than the life sentence of an individual. It was the life sentence of an entire family, of tens of thousands of guajiro families. It was the imprisonment of an entire community, of nearly all the farm families from the foothills and mountains, from Cienfuegos to Trinidad. Gabriel thought of the captives as debris swept up after a storm. The government's insistence that they were bandits made no sense. None of it made sense. Gabriel, when he looked back at his life of nearly ninety years, remembering and wondering, felt as if he had been hit by a flaming meteor. Thirty thousand, fifty thousand, seventy thousand guajiros, all trapped. And now there were more, so many more, if you counted all their children and grandchildren and great-grandchildren. The young ones didn't understand that life could be any other way, that it could be different from that lived in prison camps and captive towns.

Each morning when Gabriel awakened, he felt a brief flash of astonishment at finding that he was still alive and breathing. His dreams were luxurious ones, milking the cattle, making love to his wife, cantering across the pasture on his stallion. The smell of sugar and corn meal and manure, the sounds of cow bells and flocks of wild parrots.

Then, when he was finally awake and half-able to accept the reality of his barracoon surroundings, he would get up and eat whatever they gave him, and begin the endless task of weaving strands of dry reed into round receptacles, wondering, with each finished basket, what it was destined to hold–buttons, nuts, exotic fruit from the far north, pears and peaches and heart-shaped red or yellow apples.

Into the design of each basket Gabriel had woven one small error, a mark claiming the basket as his own. During all his years in the labor camp, no one had ever noticed his mark and Gabriel felt satisfied that at least this one secret had remained entirely his own.

It would be released, eventually, along with all the rest, all the remembered lives he carried inside his heart, his own life and the lives of his sons and daughters and grandchildren. Released, like all secrets are eventually released.

At first the boys had been kept in a fenced and guarded camp, where they were forced to construct foundations for a promised fine and modern city. Then, when the city was built, and it turned out to be nothing more than the Captive Town, they were reunited with their families and, in their new homes they tried learning to forget. They were sent out each day to work in the tobacco and cane fields, dedicating their flesh to cigars and sugar. At first there were no real roads in the city. At first it wasn't a city, but a scattering of barracoon-like houses dropped onto the countryside, immersed in dust and mud, dust in the dry season and mud during the rains, from May through October. At first there were no hospitals or schools. Taíno and the other grandchildren grew up like caged wild animals, dreaming of escape.

Amparo had escaped. They called her a gusana, a worm, but she called herself a refugee. Not an exile, but a refugee. It meant she wasn't coming back. It meant she was staying in the far North, no longer entirely Cuban. Her letters came faithfully to the prison camp by way of Isabelita, who arranged to have them smuggled in so that they wouldn't be censored.

Once, before Amparo escaped, she came to the camp to visit him, accompanied by Isabelita. After their visit, Gabriel realized that his sisters believed this was the prison. They didn't know about Boniato. They thought he had been here all along, free to circle these barracoons as he pleased, whenever he wasn't weaving the dry strands of reed and palm into secretive designs destined to receive and hold mysterious burdens in faraway lands.

He let them believe it. He didn't tell them the horrifying truths. Even if guards had not been standing around listening, he wouldn't have told. His sisters were old and carried enough sorrow around on their faces without his adding the terrible daily details of Boniato. Let them believe these camps were the prisons. Let them believe these Captive Towns, too numerous to count, were the worst of what the swept-up guajiro families had experienced.

And the worst was not yet over. As Gabriel circled the last barrack, he came around the corner to face a reptile-green truck, with its armed guards and rumbling engine. They ushered him in and he went without protest, headed once again toward the head of the alligator, this time toward the remote village where Daniel was excavating Indian ruins and cimarrón villages.

———∿———

I reached Trinidad more exhausted than I had ever been, drained by the consideration of possibilities. Cuba had grown into a burden, the island was too heavy for me. Miguelito's sorrow was too much weight for my shoulders and arms. I turned it all loose, the island, my cousin, the Captive Towns. I watched it float up toward the angels.

Suddenly I felt exhilarated. After thirty-one years, I had finally managed to climb back onto the soft belly of this alligator, with its great network of limestone caverns and underground streams snaking their way through the medieval town of Trinidad, and out to sea. Returning to Trinidad was like looking into a window, facing my childhood. The houses, some nearly five-centuries-old, had not been altered except for occasional coats of bright yellow, blue or pink paint. The doors were still ornately carved wood, the windows tall, protected by decorative wrought-iron bars. Women still leaned out against the bars to flirt and chat with passing neighbors. The streets were still cobblestone. The town square was still quiet, peaceful, as if a spell had been cast, the cobblestones still traversed by men on horseback, as if machines had not yet been invented. On the outskirts of town, watchtowers built by self-appointed masters still stood ready to serve as pedestals for sentries guarding against attacks by pirates and cimarrón slaves.

I walked slowly past the old stone house where my mother was born. It had been divided into two smaller homes, half painted flamingo-pink and half cobalt-blue. An old man came out and smiled at me from the door of the house, and the neighbors came to their barred windows to watch me pass. I circled the town repeatedly, wanting to see every landmark before entering Isabelita's house. I circled a mansion where the German naturalist Alexander Von Humboldt lived in 1801 when he chose Trinidad as the heart of tropical wildlife, a place where he could go out hunting for specimens to be studied. I circled the belltower of an old church built on a street called Desengaño, the end of "deceit."

Shuddering, I passed a museum glorifying the "Struggle Against Bandits," and a wall where one of Gabriel's cousins had been shot as a warning, his corpse left out for the vultures and children.

I paced back and forth, then entered the museum. One exhibit praised the triumph of Fidel against Batista. Another acclaimed the defeat of CIA-trained Cuban exiles at Playa Girón, the Bay of Pigs. A third commemorated the "struggle against bandits and pirates" and the "cleaning up" of the Escambray Mountains and their surroundings. Weapons and other war trophies seized from the "pirates" were displayed for European tourists, who ambled through the hall appreciatively, pointing at photographs of gaunt men whose eyes refused to meet the camera. Among them I recognized Gabriel. I left the museum feeling like someone in a dream, someone beyond control.

In one way the streets had been altered. They were too quiet, too stern. Communism had taken away the singing street vendors with their baskets of wild fruit, mountain flowers and fanciful candies. As a child, when I learned about what had happened to Cuba after that summer of 1960, I could never understand why the government had banned singing. Of course, as it turned out, not all singing had been abolished. Only the singing of street vendors trying to attract householders to the barred windows of their houses, shiny coins in hand, to exchange them for fruit or flowers or tiny caged songbirds from the mountain jungles.

As I approached my great-aunt Isabelita's house, my thoughts rested on what I knew about her life since the last time I'd seen her, thirty-one years earlier. I remembered she had a kind and gentle smile, a shy smile, yet she was firm and determined, like her mother, Gabriel's mother, Miguel's mother, Daniel's mother, Amparo's mother, my great-grandmother, the woman whose portrait still gazed out of Miguelito's window in Havana. Unlike her farm-loving mother, Isabelita had not remained a *guajira* but had become a true town woman. She painted beautiful landscapes of green hills and royal palms, and she tended to her only child, Dieguito, protecting him from danger and watching him grow until he was a full-fledged communist official. It was the only safety she could provide him.

I remembered riding with Dieguito on Gabriel's high-strung horses, crashing across hot green pastures, blinded by the gnats which landed in the corners of our eyes in clouds. Dieguito was four years older than me, and he struck me as bold and unafraid, like Gabriel's grown sons. He was accustomed to visiting the farm often and he seemed free there, daring. I remembered him as a young teenager with curly hair, a wide smile and mournful eyes, mournful because his father had died young and because he was growing up as a child of the revolution, a child of war.

Now, as I approached their house, I didn't know what to expect of Isabelita and Dieguito. I knew he was married and had children. Amparo had told me the children were little, so in my bag I carried small toys to give them, little wind-up ballerina dolls with fluffy pink skirts, and cars with tiny rubber tires.

Miguelito had warned me that Dieguito had a car and was therefore undoubtedly a member of the Party. To him, that meant danger. To me, as an outsider, it meant very little. I had no more fear of a relative in the Communist Party than I did of relatives with eccentric eating habits.

I had begun to think of Miguelito as a runaway slave, afraid to whistle out loud. I pictured him hiding behind waterfalls to fool the bounty hunters into thinking he knew magic and could make himself disappear.

I had asked Miguelito to accompany me to Trinidad but he had declined vehemently, explaining that he rarely interacted with Party members even if they were relatives.

If a time of bitter vengeance came, as Miguelito had predicted, I feared that Dieguito would be one of the targets. By communist standards, he was successful, a pillar of the revolutionary community. Isabelita had made sure of that, guiding him through his teenage years never allowing him to associate with anti-Castristas, even though she herself, according to Amparo, secretly detested Fidel and had gone up into the mountains and buried all her paintings, coins and jewelry instead of turning them over to the treasure chests of the revolution. Isabelita, Amparo had told me, had a way of knowing when things were dangerous, and of keeping her son safe.

Now, as Isabelita opened her heavy wooden door and saw me standing there, dressed like a tourist, with a camera dangling from my neck and a bag full of soaps and toys, her expression was one of such astonishment that once again I felt like a traveller through time instead of space.

Isabelita embraced me and pulled me into the house. Angels hung suspended from the ceiling, waiting. The house was even more tropical, more intensely silent and captivating than I had remembered. Dieguito was there, with his curly hair and wide smile and the same mournful eyes. He was much bigger than I'd expected, not slim like Miguelito, but solid. He welcomed me just as if the decades had not separated us, just as if he had not managed to create an upside-down world where cousins feared each other.

Dieguito introduced me to his wife and children. The "little children" my grandmother had described turned out to be teenagers. I realized, sheepishly, that Amparo's memory had tricked her, freezing the children in time. I had nothing to offer them but the ballerina dolls and toy cars. Feeling foolish, I tried to explain the frozen nature of time for those living in exile. The boy stared at me as if I were a lunatic, while the girl politely admired her doll, commenting on its mechanical, twirling movement. I gave Isabelita her soaps and Dieguito his baseball cap, and I turned over the entire bag with all its combs, packets of chewing gum, and cans of condensed milk. Dieguito's wife offered milk and fruit from the countryside surrounding Trinidad. Isabelita gave me a finely crafted basket, with one small, barely-discernible error, woven into the reed and palm design, marking the basket as Gabriel's.

Soon we were seated in mahogany rocking chairs, cautiously trading memories. Dieguito started to voice small complaints, telling me that the factories were closed because fuel and raw materials weren't arriving from the Soviet Union and eastern Europe. He started to complain about shortages, leaning forward to whisper that in Cuba he couldn't even buy a single aspirin. He sounded very much like Miguelito, restless and bursting. Isabelita shushed him.

She stood and faced her son. She looked very close to tears. "You promised," she accused Dieguito, "that today we would not discuss politics. You promised we would not ruin this visit."

Dieguito raised his hands as if to defend himself from the words. "You're right," he agreed, placating his mother, "yes, that's true, we agreed the situation in Cuba cannot be explained quickly, when it has taken so many years to develop along these lines."

They led me through the house, pointing out the bed they'd made up for me and the bathroom, which now had plumbing along with the big ceramic water jars called *tinajones*, jars reminiscent of tales from the *Arabian Nights* and *Sinbad the Sailor*. I remembered hearing stories about escaped slaves who hid in the *tinajones* of sugar plantations. The jars were set out in patios to catch rain water, and if it rained unexpectedly, sometimes a hidden runaway would drown, so reluctant was he to emerge and be recaptured.

The house, like all the colonial residences of Trinidad, was built around a tiled central patio in the Moorish style. Nearly every room had three walls instead of four, with the fourth side open, facing the patio. I remembered thinking of Isabelita's half-open kitchen as the most wonderful place where anyone could possibly cook and eat their meals. Small creatures were free to wander in and out of the house. Food hung from the ceiling, suspended in baskets, gourds and string bags. I walked through the kitchen, admiring the bundles of wild fruit and tubers, breathing in the smells of dried beef, herbs and garlic. Dieguito complained that the shortages were so severe he had to travel twenty kilometers to find fresh milk and eggs yet I saw that somehow he managed to stockpile food.

The house, with its foot-thick walls, was cool and peaceful, figurines of angels dangling in every room. Outside, the air was hot and rich, humid, clinging to the scents of rain and jasmine and salt from the beach a few kilometers away.

Distant cousins began wandering in and out of the house to greet me, the men silent and suspicious, the women gracious and smiling. We sat in rocking chairs, commenting on trivial memories, as if we had centuries stretching ahead of us, abundant time to discover each other's alien experiences. The intensity of speech I'd felt in Miguelito's house was absent here, suppressed. People in Trinidad had access to fruit from the countryside but they seemed even more frightened than those in Havana, their voices more trapped.

Gradually, small complaints seeped out of the women, the absence of soap and razor blades, the prohibition of small, harmless acts of faith.

"I remember Christmas," one of the older cousins sighed. "And Easter."

Someone else complained that now the children had to spend vacations doing volunteer work in the fields. She rolled her eyes to show that the word volunteer, for her, had a special meaning. "If they don't do it," she explained with an exaggerated sidelong glance, "it can cause big problems."

The conversation went on without me, everyone sharing a tiny complaint or two. I scanned the room, counting more than thirty portraits of Fidel, Che, Camilo, and other heroes of the revolution. Isabelita had sealed the room with portraits, insuring her son's position in the community, guaranteeing his safety. Yet she also had her figurines of angels. And one old wooden image of Jesus on the Cross.

The talk turned to travel, and soon I was aware that nearly everyone in the room was expressing a desire to flee. "We are afraid," all my distant cousins confided. I was helpless. Even if I had enough money to pay for their arrangements, most were young and able-bodied and would be unable to obtain permission from the Cuban government. Isabelita rescued me from the pain of being unable to help. She fetched a mountain of photographs bundled in yellowed paper. "These," she announced, "are your grandmother's. When she left, it was in a hurry, and she entrusted them to me. I promised I would keep them for her. Here," Isabelita said, fingering the old black-and-white prints, "is my sister's entire lifetime." She handed me the mountain of photographs, and I rested it on my lap, my eyes sifting the images. I recognized myself as a small child, my mother, my grandmother, Miguel, Daniel, Gabriel and a handful of their dead brothers and sisters.

"Do you think," Isabelita asked, gripping two edges of a table as if she feared my answer. "Do you think you might possibly take one or two of them back to her?"

I looked up at my great-aunt. She seemed so troubled. "Of course," I said, "why not? I'll take them all, the whole bundle."

Isabelita and Dieguito exchanged glances. Why were they surprised?

"You can really take them?" Dieguito demanded in a hushed voice. I nodded. Apparently he was surprised that I could travel without restrictions, carrying any sort of luggage I fancied. I began to realize that he had heard a lot of strange tales about life in the U.S.

He reached into the bundle and extracted a large black-and-white print of my uncle Juan standing next to Fidel Castro, posing with the Olympic team.

"I know you couldn't take this one," Dieguito said, grinning with nervous satisfaction. "I know that in the North they don't like him, and you could get in trouble for carrying this." Suddenly I felt very sorry for my communist cousin. He had been deceived. He thought the U.S. was just as restrictive as Cuba.

"I can take anything I want," I explained, deciding to be brutally frank about rules in the North. "Certainly any photographs. We don't have censorship."

I found a faded gray image of Gabriel standing in his corral, shaking a fist at the devil, his smile vibrant, exultant, cattle in the background, hills, scattered palms.

"What happened?" I asked Dieguito, holding up the image.

My cousin stood and slashed his hands across the air in front of his chest, with a vehement slicing motion that meant 'finished.' "Gone," he said, his voice trembling, "*No existe.*"

It was the same answer I always received in Cuba. *No existe.* It doesn't exist. I knew Gabriel was dead. I knew the farm was in government hands. I knew Gabriel's descendants were prisoners in the Captive Town. And yet, there was still something which did exist, and no one was willing to discuss its presence. I accepted Dieguito's denial and wrapped up all the photographs for delivery to my exiled grandmother.

Everyone had fallen silent. All the distant cousins had drifted into different rooms or, back out to the street, to their own houses. Dieguito's wife was busy preparing a meal of rice, black beans, plantains, strong coffee and fruit with cheese. I knew I was about to consume a generous portion of the family's monthly rations.

Isabelita followed me as I paced the open kitchen, pausing below each angel, looking up to see if I could detect anything more than a figurine, hushed wings and whispered melodies.

"Do you think," my great-aunt asked cautiously, "that they open the mail?"

I was startled. For several decades she had been sending letters to my grandmother, uncertain whether Cuban officials were going to inspect what she wrote. "Yes," I said grimly, "they do open the letters." I hesitated. "Sometimes," I finally added, "a letter comes from Cuba with a stamp on the inside. Or with the bottom of the envelope slit open."

Her eyes grew round and sorrowful. "On the inside!" she echoed. "Aah!" Dieguito approached his mother, and the two of them stood silently gazing at each other, thinking of all the years and all the carefully worded letters.

I imagined that my great-aunt must have been thinking she was right all along to be so cautious. She had never felt safe receiving telephone calls from Amparo in the U.S. and, finally, one day when both sisters were very old, she'd told my grandmother to stop calling because it could cause big problems for her son. Receiving too many phone calls from the U.S., Isabelita told Amparo, made the entire household a target of suspicion.

We sat down to the feast Dieguito's wife had prepared. The distant cousins were still complaining of shortages. I ate as if I had been deprived for years, as if I were the one accustomed to sparse rations.

After dinner I stepped out into the patio's glaring heat, where a bright green lizard clung to the side of an old well. I knew the well. It pumped from an underground river in the caverns beneath Trinidad. The lizard bobbed its head up and down in a rigid, stilted manner, like a dancing marionette.

Tiny, colorful songbirds fluttered in bamboo cages hanging from the branches of a mango tree planted in a patch of soil exposed between broken tiles. In one corner of the patio there were *tinajones* filled with rain water, and three Taíno stools of dark gray stone. Each stool had four legs and a concave seat. I walked across the patio and sat on one of the stools, surprised to find that even though it was many centuries old, the seat was still very comfortable. Remembering what Daniel had told Gabriel about

Taíno stools, I guessed that the stone seat must have been carved for a *cacique*, one of the chiefs who ruled the peaceful Cuban Indians until the Spaniards came along like meteorites, crashing onto the island.

Dieguito followed me out onto the patio, smiling. Abruptly, I became aware of an evil presence on the tiles between us. A large snarling demon crouched beside me. Dieguito walked right past it without noticing, and came to sit with me on one of his Taíno stools.

"You know," he said, "my mother is very upset. Now that she sees how easily you can take Amparo's photographs to the U.S., my mother wonders whether maybe you could have done the same with Juan's poems. You know we burned his poems, don't you? It was his last request before he left for the North. My mother cried and cried while she was burning those poems. I was very young then, but I remember how she cried. And I read some of the poems before they crinkled up. They weren't anything danger-ous, just verses about love and other ordinary things. Juan didn't want to leave them though. Just in case, you know? Sometimes if they find some-thing like that in your house after you leave, they take it out on your rela-tives. Tell me," Dieguito asked, "would you have been allowed to take Juan's poems with you to the U.S. if we hadn't burned them?"

I nodded, paralyzed with fear. The fear felt like opium, a suspension of the movement of blood in my veins. At my side, the demon bared its fangs and crept forward.

Suddenly we heard a squeal from Dieguito's daughter. "Uncle Daniel is here!" she shouted.

"Yes," I answered Dieguito quickly, "yes, I could have taken poems. Poetry isn't dangerous, not dangerous at all."

———⌀———

On the evening of his rebellion, Taíno set out striding across a field of smoldering cane stubble, remembering how it felt to be tossed into the sky, remembering something his grandfather had told him that morning by the river as they watched the reflections of palms. From each generation, Gabriel had explained, God chooses a few who can never stop remembering.

Taíno could barely recall the appearance of the farm but he remembered the feel of mud crusted onto his feet and calves, the music of frogs and parrots, the taste of sugar sucked from the hard fibers of cane.

One of the wild parrots had stayed behind when its flock clattered away, spinning and dipping through the sky, screeching. The abandoned bird dwelled on the thatched roof of Gabriel's bohío, learning to imitate the words of people passing below. Sometimes Taíno would gaze up into the thatch and the parrot would cock its head and repeat, in a misted echo of a woman's voice, "Oh, how pretty," or "Not again!" or "If God wills."

So Taíno started repeating whatever the bird said and soon they were both saying "If God wills," just the way Gabriel's wife said it whenever she wished for anything. Taíno would sit on the clean-swept earth floor and gaze up into the thatch with its maze of wasp's nests and slivers of light from the sky beyond, and the boy would talk to the parrot, asking it questions, always receiving the same memorized answers.

Then that morning came along, and the men dressed in crocodile skins tossed Taíno into the sky and he came down captive, and one of the last things he saw, before the truck rumbled away with him and all the others trapped in its bowels, was his parrot flying away from the burning thatch, shrieking, "If God wills."

Taíno remembered waking up in a big fancy house surrounded by women who never stopped crying. He remembered the guards who wouldn't let him go outside and warned him about standing near open windows.

He stood near the windows anyway and gazed out at the sea wall, and beyond it, the sea and above it, the sky, with seagulls and angular black frigate birds looking like stitches in a blue cloth, and the clouds, hurled to shore every afternoon, crashing against waves.

Green trucks rumbled along the street carrying work brigades out to the fields. Sometimes a truck would stop and everyone would get out and throw rocks at Taíno's window, shouting "Parasite, worm, imperialist dog!" Taíno would duck, and run to ask his grandmother what the words meant and Gabriel's wife, who couldn't stop crying, just embraced her grandson and told him to stay away from the window because there was no explanation for the ways of madmen.

Taíno would wait until the trucks passed and then he crept back to the window, hoping to glimpse a sailboat beyond the sea wall, with its white triangles which resembled folded wings.

He grew up remembering the lost-bird farm and the folded-wing sea and when he was a man and wanted to stop remembering, he couldn't. By then the women had stopped crying, and the men had stopped raging, and everyone lived in the Captive Town without talking much about the past or the future, about the farm or the sea or the sky.

Taíno's steps carried him across field after field of smoldering cane and he wondered how long it would be before soldiers pursued him across the fields and found him hiding under the mogotes, in the caves, ready to die for his memory, for those flashes of illusion that came racing through his mind like fireflies.

Taíno tried to remember whether it was his grandfather Gabriel or his uncle Daniel who'd first told him that both the Indians and the Africans had been in the habit of assigning to a few men from each generation the task of remembering.

When the crocodile-men took him out of the big house called Look-at-the-Sea, and moved him to the Captive Town on the tail of the alligator, Taíno had expected to be swallowed by water. Sooner or later, he'd thought, the alligator will thrash its fierce tail and everyone will fall off into the sea. The people from the lost-bird farm moved into a new town built by all the fathers who kept calling it Captive Town until the name stuck and when Taíno was older and he asked his father to explain why he'd helped build a captive town, his father had answered that sometimes in life there are no choices.

Later Taíno understood that his father had been kept inside a fenced concentration camp on the tail of the alligator and that the fence itself was enough to make a man build the town which will become his children's captor.

Taíno grew up in the Captive Town and at first the crocodile-men stood guard, making sure the people from the lost-bird farm went out every day to till the soil of tobacco fields and cane fields. When the crocodile-men looked at Taíno they had a way of knowing that he couldn't stop remembering and they treated him more harshly than the rest. But eventually most of them went away and, even without all the crocodile-men and fences, the people from the lost-bird farm knew they couldn't leave their Captive Town. Taíno thought of his family as people without feet.

When the people of the lost farms were finally allowed to build their own schools, Taíno tried to pay attention but by then he was big and rebellious and his school file was stamped "indifferent to socialism." Taíno knew it didn't matter because all the men in his family carried identification cards that marked them as inheritors of the Captive Town. The entire island knew that when rebellion came, it would come from the heart of the lost ones who still yearned for their farms.

Taíno remembered working in the tobacco fields, bending over the plants with their big, floppy leaves, surrounded by time and space, inhaling the bitterness of his memory. He cursed the men who would smoke his flesh in the form of a cigar. They would be Party members or rich igno-rant foreigners with no way of knowing that their cigars were crafted of human flesh. Taíno imagined that someday his flesh would travel across the sea, trapped inside the tobacco leaves, vanishing in smoke and flame.

From his brief journey through school, Taíno remembered only fragments. School was designed for the children of crocodile-men, not for the lost-bird inheritors of memory. Taíno remembered that once a teacher had loaned him a book, by the Argentine poet Jorge Luis Borges, a brief tale about a ruined city which continued to exist only because one wild horse remembered its location.

Taíno remembered that tale and the description of a blue house inhabited by the Chilean poet and communist, Pablo Neruda. An intensely blue house overlooking the sea, a house filled with carved wooden figureheads retrieved from shipwrecks, a house with colored glass bottles tumbled by waves, a house where, mysteriously, sea shells had become imbedded in the floorboards and ceiling.

In school, when Taíno learned about Neruda's house, he imagined it was a place where people could breathe even though they were immersed in the depths of the sea.

"I love your hands hurt by the sea, your hair motionless over eyes that scan the round horizon." Taíno read the verse by Neruda and imag-ined that the poet must have fallen in love with one of his wounded fig-ureheads, some carved wooden female washed into the blue house by tumbling waves.

The figureheads were all named. Marie Celeste, Guillermina, Jenny Lind, La Micaela, La Novia. During cold winters, condensation collect-ed in the eyes of Marie Celeste and tears streamed down her face, so that she appeared to weep. Crowds of pilgrims came to the house of the poet who believed in miracles.

If the miracles had not already convinced Taíno that people were guided by something beyond their own ideas, then the poet's bathroom would have convinced him beyond a doubt. Inside the bowl of his toilet, Neruda had painted flowers. When Taíno read about the blue house with its weeping statue and its decorated toilet bowl, he felt a pounding of sheer joy, knowing that he was right and the crocodile-men were wrong, because communists were not supposed to crave flowers inside their toilet bowls.

Taíno learned that Neruda kept a fishing boat on the patio outside his kitchen. When friends visited, the poet would climb into his boat with them and, they would all pretend to be sailing away from the blue house by the sea.

Taíno longed to sail away from the Captive Town. He was tired of pretending. He was tired of the weariness, the melancholy. He felt like the women of his family must have felt when they had to wear mourning for twenty consecutive years. Taíno remembered thinking that the women must have grown angry when the men kept killing themselves, one after the other, as if the act of suicide were some sort of contagious disease.

Taíno thought of his heart as a root in the earth, absorbing dissolved sorrow until it entered his veins and solidified as debris. He longed to sail away from the island clinging to one of those white triangles of folded wing. Whenever he thought about his life in the Captive Town, Taíno suspected that, if he had sailed away, he would have developed a fear of islands. He would have searched out some immense land to dwell on, some vast desert or endless prairie where no one could build four walls around you and label them Look-at-the-Sea.

Taíno was racing from field to field now, fragments of his grandfather's rhymed songs floating into his memory through the movement of his feet. Songs about the blood-red farm and the child sent soaring across an expanse of sky.

Taíno hurried along a trail between two burning cane fields, remembering. Creeping between the charred stalks, he headed for the tobacco fields with their wide bitter leaves. The sun had set. Now he could walk all night. He could run. There would be steep jungle on the mogotes and below them caverns, underground rooms big enough to hide an army.

By now his wife would be in one of those vast distant lands. Taíno remembered his wife with the anguish of a new loss. She had stepped into the shadow of one of those triangular folded wings and, the wind had carried her away. She'd left the island the way hope left, clinging to a folded wing, dodging the storms and sharks.

She'd wanted him to go. For years she had been saying it aloud, risking imprisonment even for voicing the wish. She was like him, a child of the Captive Town. She said there was nothing to lose. But Taíno couldn't abandon the island. He couldn't stop remembering.

So instead he'd gathered the tools of rebellion, and now he was nearing the end, whistling a tune he'd learned from his uncle Miguel, something about flying.

———— ᨳ ————

Daniel stepped into the quiet patio, and moved toward my resting place on the carved Taíno stool. In its bamboo cage, a tiny blue *azulejo* bird sang. Beside me, the demon crouched and snarled. Dieguito was telling me about the accomplishments of the revolution, describing the clinics and rural schools.

I didn't recognize Daniel. He looked much younger than his nearly ninety years. His appearance was one of quiet dignity and strength. Gone was the passionate young rebel who'd hidden under a *ceiba* tree in defiance of Machado's secret police, yet something of the courage gained from that rebellion had become ingrained in the old man's demeanor. I looked at my great-uncle, and saw that he still carried himself with the humility of his *guajiro* childhood, even though he'd left the cane fields and cattle behind and had become an internationally respected archaeologist, known for his excavations of the remains of villages, Taíno, *cimarrón* and *conquistador*. A part of Daniel seemed to have stayed in the past.

The patio was so hot and so peaceful, so filled with sunlight and the scent of mangos, that I felt myself carried inland, to the only place I could never reclaim, that farm just a few leagues away, the farm with all its sugar and milk, frogs and worms.

I watched the demon slink away. The songbird continued its serenade, and from my stool I could see into all the open rooms surrounding the patio, the kitchen with its mounds of fruit, the parlor with Isabelita's collection of white porcelain angels dangling from the ceiling. I felt like I had been sitting in that spot for a thousand years. Nothing had changed except Daniel.

The blue songbird sang from its tiny bamboo cage. Daniel started talking, and after a moment of formality and greeting; he began to pour out every detail of Gabriel's life, even down to the bird calls used by Alzados as they communicated with other rebels in the mountains, calling across rocky places where escaped slaves had once gathered wild honey for trade with the pirates, who gave them, in exchange for the honey, gold coins which could never be spent, but were buried in the mountains.

Hearing about Gabriel's last free morning, when he wandered down to the river with his grandson, I felt wistful and confused. I wanted to tell Daniel about Miguelito's silence and his yearning to sing, but Daniel lived far from Miguelito, and couldn't help him. He couldn't help Gabriel's sons and grandsons either. They lived far away, in one of the Captive Towns on the tail of the alligator. Daniel said the people of the Captive Towns were not formally recognized by the Cuban government as political prisoners, and as a result, could never emigrate, not even when occasional amnesty programs allowed others to leave.

Thinking of Gabriel's captive family and of Juan's burnt poems, I gathered together all the distant cousins and photographed them in the patio, along with Isabelita and Daniel, Dieguito, his wife and children, the *tinajones* and Taíno stools, the porcelain figurines of angels, even the snarling demon which had returned to the patio and sat drooling under the bright blue songbird in its bamboo cage.

Everyone expressed delight at seeing a camera in action after so many years of prohibitions against outdoor photography, which, combined with the scarcity of film and absence of developing services, had turned Cuba into an island devoid of the preserved images we in the North are accustomed to possessing, cold but precious images frozen in time.

I searched the house and patio for angels but, there were only the porcelain figurines and the demon, a real demon, breathing, snarling and threatening to attack.

Taíno bent down over a tiny flame, and peered at the flash of light as it began to spread. With satisfaction, he straightened his back and raised one fist, shaking it. He grinned, knowing his enemy was out on

the horizon somewhere, dressed in reptile-green.

He hurried to the next field, a trace of gasoline spilling from the can he carried. It was nearly empty. Just a few more carefully rationed sparks, and then his flight to the caves.

Lately he'd been having strange dreams. One about a slave woman named Dulce, sweet like sugar, but tricked by her master into cooking the flesh of her own son after his leg was chopped off as punishment for trying to run away. Another about soldiers patrolling an island where all the rivers flowed uphill. Shoulder to shoulder, the soldiers marched in an endless sinuous line, past rivers rushing up, up, up, into the mountains, and from there to the clouds.

When she sailed away, Taíno's wife was pregnant. Now he wondered whether his child existed yet in some vast distant land, or submerged in the sea. He wondered whether it had turned out to be a boy or a girl.

On the night of her departure, Taíno dreamed that he and his wife lived on the tail of an alligator. When the beast moved, he had to climb inside to keep from falling off. There he was wrapped in the intestines, among fragments of human limbs the animal had consumed.

Taíno now walked very quickly, scanning the horizon, field after field, the towering cane and floppy tobacco, the sky, wondering how one man could hold so many millions of people hostage, thinking that the gasoline and the flame were just symbols and mattered little. His only real defense was remembering.

Taíno began whispering to himself as he walked. Suddenly he felt small and frightened. He thought about a time when he was very little and his aunt Amparo came to the farm and told him he would forget everything about his childhood, and then, when he was older, it would all start to seep back into his heart, bit by bit, flashing into his mind like fireflies.

Amparo had said that when she was nearly sixty she suddenly remembered dancing at the age of two, dancing with all her guajiro uncles and cousins who had come to the farm to help build a corral. "They always brought their guitars with them in those days," Amparo had said wistfully. "Just in case the work day became a day of celebration instead. And it did, in those days, often enough."

Taíno had often looked forward to that sudden reclaiming of memory described by his aunt. He anticipated the day when he would be very old and suddenly, without effort, the clarity of that morning would return and, through sky and smoke, he would finally understand what had happened when he returned from the green river with his grandfather, and found the farm burning and the parrot escaping. Now, as he set the fields aflame, Taíno knew he would never recapture that delayed release of memory.

He turned onto a muddy trail, humming uncle Miguel's tune about flying. He imagined himself soaring above the fields and the trail, lifted above the red soil which loved sugar and above the black soil which loved tobacco.

Then he sang another of Miguel's songs about the Taíno legend of the sun and about a man made by the sun, a man who was lonely until he found a woman made by the moon and, about their son whose very existence infuriated the man. The man was jealous of his wife's love for the baby. The man seized his baby and carried it up into the mountains, leaving it there to starve. When the baby was dead, the man went back and hid its tiny body inside a gourd. The woman wandered all over the mountains searching for her child, and when she passed by the gourd, a small shiny black bird pointed it out to her. She peered into the gourd, and out came rivers, fish, turtles, and all the waters of the world, with all the sea creatures, a flood which left the land surrounded, an island.

Taíno continued his pilgrimage of fire, ending the rhymed Taíno Indian legend, then singing one about the soldiers of Imperial Spain, who forced Cuban guajira women to dance, and then, as they danced, executed them. Taíno grasped that image of the dancing women, the women flying away from the horror, floating away, twirling away, carried by wind and fire. Singing about fire, Taíno was reminded of his immediate task, burning the sugar to keep him the Maximum Leader, from exporting its sweetness and selling it for a profit just as if he were not really a communist. And he wasn't. Taíno had realized that when he was still very young. He wasn't any of the things he claimed to be. Not even a communist. Fragment by fragment, the island had been sold, first the sugar, then the cattle and, all along, year after year, the people.

Taíno had chopped enough cane to build a tower reaching the stars. Fidel had tended so much tobacco that he felt his flesh becoming smoke. The sugar had been brought brought to Spain by Moors and to Cuba by Columbus. The tobacco was already there on the island, flaming from the nose and mouth and ears of the Taíno, Siboney and Guanahacabibe as they enjoyed the peaceful stretches of time between hurricanes, meteorites and raids by cannibals.

Taíno paced the moonless night, surrounded by field after field of tobacco and cane, his gasoline can empty and discarded, the new fields left standing, the smoldering ones far behind now. He knew he must be getting close to the caverns, to the black gaping entrance of whatever was hidden below. Traveling underground, he could reach the mogotes, he could dwell beneath the sheer cliffs, the towering jungles, the galloping clouds. He would emerge at night to find food and firewood. He would need nothing else.

Dieguito took me on a walking tour of Trinidad's clinics and schools, built by the revolutionary government. Until now Dieguito had seemed nearly as restless as Miguelito. His memory was filled with forbidden treasures, Taíno artifacts, buried coins, porcelain angels, a portrait of Jesus and the trickling streams of small complaints against shortages and hypocrisy.

But now he showed me how serenely the children of Trinidad rested on rows of cots inside a clean and modern child care center. I expressed admiration. Dieguito was satisfied. He had done his duty. We walked along the cobblestone streets, visiting distant cousins and enjoying quaint views from hillsides and church belltowers. Then we made our way back to Isabelita's house, dodging a cluster of French tourists who were busy trying to peer into the parlor through a tall ornately barred window.

Isabelita and Daniel were seated in massive rocking chairs, quietly discussing the price of black-market meat. I joined them, and Dieguito's wife quietly brought me a *mamonsillo* fresh from the trees of some local collective farm. This fruit, I thought, biting into the flesh, might be the fruit of that same tree I ate from on Gabriel's farm exactly thirty-one years ago, to the day, the hour, the instant.

From the top of the lanky tree, Gabriel's grown sons had tossed down small round pieces of the sky, which I caught and ate, standing far below them, barefoot, toes in the worm-infested soil, eyes lifted toward the heights of this tree where my cousins touched the sky.

Now I spat a large round seed into my palm and went in search of a trash bin in the open kitchen. Angels were hovering all over the house, humming and waiting. Real angels, not the porcelain figurines. Where had they been before? Present, but quiet, so that I couldn't hear their song?

I snooped around the kitchen, but found no garbage container, so I stepped out into the patio, through the wall which, in the half-open rooms of Isabelita's house, did not exist. The demon was glaring at the kitchen, at the angels. It had retreated into the shelter of a woodpile, and lay sulking next to the bright green lizard, which sunned itself nearby.

I planted the *mamonsillo* seed in a patch of red mud between broken tiles, then returned to the parlor, where Isabelita asked me to show her a coin from the North. She said she was curious about our lives, our surroundings, the things we held in our hands, in our thoughts, in our hearts.

My great-aunt followed me, asking why her sister never visited. I explained that the Cuban government placed severe restrictions on visits by relatives from the U.S. Isabelita's optimistic expression faded into one of shock and dismay.

"In order to visit you," I told my great-aunt, in response to her timid questions about travel restrictions, "my grandmother would have to file for a Cuban passport, even though she has been a U.S. citizen for many years. She would, in essence, become Cuban again, and that would make her vulnerable. She would be afraid of..."

Of what? Of becoming trapped again, of being held on the island against her will. Of becoming a person who would burn poetry. Of being blamed for the crimes of dissident cousins. Of being expected to inform to the secret police, to inform on neighbors, friends, cousins. ...

"She would be afraid," I concluded, deciding to leave to Isabelita's imagination what was the nature of her fears. My great-aunt seemed to age as I spoke. I wondered if she knew that in 1980 the flight of more than one hundred thousand *"Marielito"* refugees had been blamed on the influence of Cuban-American relatives who had visited the island, bringing images of abundance, safety and freedom of speech.

"The U.S. government," I explained, "prohibits only ordinary tourism to Cuba. It's part of the economic boycott. U.S. citizens aren't allowed to spend money in Cuba. But I have an exemption. The U.S. doesn't restrict visits to relatives. Only the Cuban government limits the possibility of visiting.

"The Cuban government," I continued quietly, remembering that we had to be careful in case neighbors were listening through the windows, "allows only fifty Cuban-Americans to visit relatives in Cuba each week." Fifty to visit nearly eleven million. How many times had I tried to get my name placed on that waiting list and been refused because there were already several tens of thousands ahead of me, because I was related to Gabriel. I explained that relatives could visit only by making arrangements with Marazul, "The Blue Sea," an official Cuban government travel agency with branches in Miami and New York. I had been calling Marazul for years, and the secretaries had been hanging up on me for years, insisting that it would be absolutely impossible for me to ever visit relatives in Cuba.

As I spoke to Isabelita, her face crumpled. "I have been trying for many years to arrange this visit," I told her. "On and off for twenty years."

Taíno found the cave and entered. He crouched on a ledge of translucent stone, wondering how long it would take the soldiers to find him and he wondered whether anyone beyond the island knew about the Captive Towns, about men like Gabriel.

Whenever Taíno thought of his grandfather, anger brewed like thick coffee, served bitter, without the sugar. Gabriel had died at Daniel's house, hundreds of miles away, on the remote head of the alligator. They had finally released him, after three decades of prison and forced labor, and they had sent him away just in time to die. On the tail of the alligator, in the Captive Town, Gabriel's wife had died also, as soon as she heard about her husband's last transfer, as soon as she understood, finally and without recourse, that the man she had been waiting for would never be allowed to live with her again, but would be kept separate and distant. Taíno remembered how his grandmother had died of yearning, of sorrow and disappointment. A bullet could not have acted more swiftly.

Taíno sat on the crystal ledge, wondering whether he was truly as isolated as he felt, wondering whether anyone knew, whether anyone would ever know, whether in the North or at the bottom of the sea, wondering if his vanished wife and new child would ever know, whether anyone would remember. He fell asleep, resting his head on the stone, dreaming about bearded soldiers who peeled off their reptile skins and hung them on hooks behind doors.

I embraced my great-aunt and, feeling embarassed but satisfied, told her, "You won't be forgotten." Soon after, while I was standing in the patio watching a battle between angels and demons, a Cubatur guide caught up with me. She was furious, scolding me for leaving my tour group. The pretty guide said I could have run into problems, I should be careful in a place where I didn't know how things worked. She said, "Didn't I tell you that as long as you're in Cuba, you're my responsibility?" She was cordial, solicitous, protective. She told me the Cuban government had only my best interests at heart. I was immediately ushered away from Trinidad, flown to Havana, and then, the next day, after receiving several hours of honeyed speeches by smiling guides, I was sent away from the island on a plane which reminded me of slave legends about flying.

They rushed me away, shut inside the roaring silver body of an old Soviet Aeroflot jet. As I was deported, the green island grew smaller. It was an island I now knew, with certainty, was truly enchanted, an island blessed and cursed and bewitched, an island shaped like a sleeping dragon.

The plane flew head-on into a storm, slamming against the clouds, battered by wind. I thought my life was ending. Hours later, I arrived in Mexico City, alive, but frantic with fear.

In their effort to keep my departure quiet and friendly, the guides hadn't checked my luggage. I still had my grandmother's old photographs, even the big one of my uncle Juan posing with his Olympic team, next to a smiling black-and-white image of the Maximum Leader. And I had Gabriel's imperfect basket, and the stored-up fragments of his released memory and a few verses of Miguelito's songs, a few gentle melodies.

Taíno's eyes drifted open and, in the pale round beam cast by a green soldier's flashlight, he recognized one of his distant cousins from Havana, a tall young man whose name he could barely remember, the brother of Araceli, a man he had seen only in pictures carried around by

Daniel whenever he visited the Captive Town, saying he wanted to teach all the separated cousins to recognize each other.

The soldier leaned forward to inspect Taíno's face, then whispered something to his companion and, all Taíno could hear was the single word "Comrades" followed by a blur of sound and then finally "mi primo", my cousin.

Taíno realized that he had been recognized and, startled, he stood up, hitting his head against the stone of the cave, wishing he had gone farther into its depths right away, suddenly seeing that yes, he was afraid of death after all.

He remembered the homemade explosive device in his pocket and saw that now it would be useless. He had planned to destroy the soldiers when they came to arrest him. He knew they would come. He knew it all along. He planned it. He longed for it, for them to come and arrest him and, instead of carrying him off to prison, for them, the soldiers, to be destroyed in the cave along with him. But he hadn't guessed that among the soldiers sent to arrest him he would recognize a cousin and that the cousin would also recognize him.

Then he sat back down facing the horrifying truth. All of this had been done in memory of his family, or so he had imagined and, now he would be unable to go through with it. His rebellion had been defeated. Not by force but by recognition.

The cave was filled with a flurry of wings and, everyone, even Taíno, assumed that they were the foul wings of bats.

When I returned from Cuba, I tried to tell people what it was like but, my words sounded so strange and remote that nearly everyone stared at me blankly, as if I had chronicled a journey to Neptune or Saturn, as if I had tried to describe the colors of gaseous rings or the patterns of light and dark inside the craters of distant moons. I might as well have said I'd been hit by a meteor. Northerners said they couldn't imagine a land where people were afraid of their own brothers and cousins, where feeling unhappy was against the law, and wistful songs were considered dangerous. They said they couldn't imagine the fear, the silence, the constant search for food, the storm of melancholy sweeping across an entire island, the loss of one's own voice, the loneliness.

I became secretive. It was something I had learned on the island of sorcerers and seraphim. Nothing could be forgotten. I hoarded the memories like an escaped slave hiding pirate gold.

I asked myself questions that could never be answered. Had the guides followed me on their own or, had someone, a stranger, informed them that I wasn't an ordinary tourist, but a Cuban-American visiting relatives without the permission of Marazul? Perhaps it had been the cabdriver who'd appeared at my door during the darkest hours of the night, demanding and accepting bribes? Or perhaps the maid who claimed her name was Amparo, my grandmother's name. Or, although I dreaded the thought, perhaps some distant cousin seeking extra rations or career advancement? I would never know, and it would never matter. My message had been delivered. The treasures had been smuggled out. Now I was free. I could return to my safe, comfortable routine in that arid rural corner of a big world. I could think of Cuba as one of those places the mind creates inside the boundaries of its dreams. I could forget.

But I couldn't forget. I felt myself still immersed in the deep, all-consuming melancholy of Havana, the illusory serenity of Trinidad, even the unseen rhythm and melody of the lost farm.

I tracked the daily news for information about Cuba. One day I read that bus service was paralyzed by the fuel shortage and that carrier pigeons were transporting government messages. Oxen were plowing fields while tractors stood idle. Bicycles were so precious that at night thieves ambushed riders to seize their cycles. Streetlights were being turned off and even television viewing hours were being limited to conserve power.

A Los Angeles Times headline read, "Let them eat ice cream," telling how the sweet frozen treat was now the only abundant food in Cuba.

A soap delivery truck was hijacked for its precious cargo.

Catholic Bishops asked Fidel to legalize the public celebration of Christmas. They received no reply.

An observer from the United Nations Commission on Human Rights was denied entry to the island.

The Maximum Leader announced that the people were willing to die for their leaders.

Work crews were assigned the task of digging a network of tunnels under the city of Havana. The tunnels were intended as bomb shelters in case of an attack by the armies of the North.

I received a human rights bulletin documenting the consequences of a peaceful demonstration which had taken place in front of State Security Headquarters at Villa Marista in Havana. A coalition of dissident groups had convened to shout, "Liberty for political prisoners!" State Security's paramilitary Rapid Action Brigades swiftly disbanded the demonstrators, who were beaten, tried and sentenced without access to defense lawyers.

During the course of my safe and comfortable days, I tried to tell people about silence and fear on the island, but a pastor from one of the small country churches said, "No one gives a darn about Cuba," and a woman in the congregation said, "This is just totally depressing." And she walked away in disgust.

"But Cuba is so close!" I shouted. "What happened to 'Love thy neighbor'?" I demanded. The pastor shrugged. "Most people don't," was his matter-of-fact answer. As if to make amends, another more empathetic pastor wrote "Pray for Cuba" in his weekly church bulletin every week for a year.

So I started writing Miguelito's words and Daniel's words which had been inherited from Gabriel and, remembering my promise to Miguelito, I wrote under a false name, just as if the words were still trapped in a place where words are dangerous.

An acquaintance asked me how my life had been changed by my return to the island. At first the question perplexed me. Then I realized that the journey had made me see the North through Cuban eyes. In supermarkets I would stop and gawk at the abundance. On amusement park roller coasters I would notice the difference between the delight of simulated fear and the grim panic of true dread. I realized that the pilgrimage had changed me profoundly. Now I could truly believe the strangest statements made in the Bible. Plagues of frogs. Manna for breakfast. Burning bushes. Evil kings. Horned beasts. Detached human fingers writing prophecies on walls.

I realized that the journey had made me believe that truth exists and that it is absolute, even when kept secret.

I continued scanning the human rights bulletins. A coalition for democracy had convened in Havana's Church of the Virgin of Mercy to pray for the liberty of political prisoners. The leaders were arrested by State Security while thousands of worshipers continued praying.

Like the Cuban teenagers in their stripped-bare churches, I tried to pray for Fidel, for guidance for him from above. A repentant slave trader wrote the hymn "Amazing Grace." The blind see. The lost are found. Couldn't the evil king also be saved? Yet I continued to think of him as suicidal. Any day now he might leap into the sea, trying to drag nearly eleven million captives down with him. He was becoming a giant octopus, a sea serpent. I prayed for armies of angels.

Then I received the bulletin about the arrest and torture of Omar, cousin of my grandmother Amparo and of Gabriel, Miguel, Isabelita and Daniel. Omar, the brother of Alvaro who, even though his flesh was crawling with maggots when they pulled him out of the punishment cells, survived to tell his cousin Gabriel about the *Alzados* . Omar, brother of Emilio and Adán who had risen up in arms so briefly and had been shot as examples, Emilio in the mountains, and Adán in the town square of Trinidad, a corpse left on the cobblestones for all the children to see.

All my life, questions of good and evil always appeared to be centered in Cuba. Was God like nature? Was Fidel an idealist gone mad or a madman gone evil or an ordinary *Santero* who danced too well and became possessed by demons?

"We thought he was God," Gabriel had said of Fidel. But God is loving.

I bought a red mare and, every day, while my husband was at work in the fields and my children were at school, I cantered back and forth across dry slopes and irrigated orchards, thinking of Omar and of his arrest on charges of being in a "dangerous" state of mind. I felt that the word described my own state.

At night I dreamed of Cuban women standing awestruck in front of supermarket bins filled with apples and guavas. I dreamed about Cuban teenagers singing along with wandering pastors, waving their hands toward God as if to say, "Look, here we are, down here!"

I dreamed I was roaming the countryside near Trinidad, and just when I was about to find the lost farm, the Maximum Leader, appeared wearing the flashy costume of a Las Vegas performer, smirking and smiling, claiming he would create a New Man who would live in paradise. In the dream, someone laughed and I awakened, certain that I had heard the devil.

I dreamed I was climbing down a steep cliff on the island, trying to reach the shore of the sea, intending to collect fragile seashells as they were washed onto the beach by shimmering waves. I was anticipating the cool smooth touch of pale yellow moon snails marked with delicate brown spirals, as if the shells had been painted by a careful hand.

Descending the cliff, I noted with alarm that the ocean was rising fast, surging against the cliff in great ominous waves. I clambered back up the precipice and, reaching the summit, I saw a panorama of the most exquisitely beautiful green farm imaginable—with hills, cane, cattle, flowers, butterflies, a *guajiro* working in the fields, singing and waving his woven-palm hat toward the vibrant sky.

I felt like I was in heaven. For days after the dream of a rescued farm, I went about my ordinary tasks feeling thrilled, intensely hopeful and content, singing.

It was autumn, fire season. Seated on the back of my mare I galloped across the dry hills, savoring the dream-image of that free *guajiro* on his reclaimed land.

I wrote to Miguelito and Aurora, trying to describe the seasons, the fires, the roadrunners, bobcats and coyotes, the trap-door spiders and horned lizards, the turquoise sky.

At first I received cautiously self-censored notes. We are fine. Everyone is well. The weather is lovely.

If only we had agreed on secret code words to transport truths past the eyes and fingers of Cuban government censors!

Miguelito wrote asking for guitar strings, and as I packaged and sent them, I felt a sense of dismay. Why hadn't I thought of sending guitar strings without being asked? How could I be so oblivious?

The next letter I received from my cousin said, "I hope you feel like a human being," and from those secretive words I knew he must mean that he did not feel human. Another letter came and, from the bitter emptiness between cautious, self-censored words, I knew he had finally given up the masquerade, the daily routine of his government job. He was singing.

I searched the news information about the suffering of Cuban dissidents, the crackdown against protest, the repression of poetry and art. Other topics seemed to be occupying the minds of reporters from the U.S. who had drifted into the past. They wrote nostalgic pieces about the Missile Crisis. They reported that historians were arguing about Columbus, some vowing that he was a good man, a devout man, a man of vision. Others retorting that he threatened to slice out the tongues of his sailors if they denied that Cuba was Asia. They said that eventually he was recalled by the Spanish monarchs because he persisted in enslaving baptized Indians, defying the expressed orders of the rulers of Imperial Spain. Power had seeped into the man's soul, one historian insisted, corrupting him.

I began searching obscure libraries for clues to decipher Gabriel's memory. Through an interlibrary loan I found a list of Alzados killed in the Escambray Mountains and in Trinidad between 1960 and 1966. The list included the names of many of my distant cousins. Emilio and Adán. Nicomedes, Adonis, Elizardo, Ibrahím, Angel, Efraín, Noel.

Christmas came and, the Soviet Union was dissolved. Cuba stood trembling on the brink of rebellion. My husband and children surprised me with a kite-shaped pendant of polished lapis flecked with gold. It made me think of sailboats, of the sky and the tides.

We walked to a stable at a nearby feed store to enjoy a living Nativity Scene featuring shepherds from a local children's choir. The shepherds were dressed in bathrobes, with striped towels tied onto their heads. While Mary was still on her donkey, it bucked. The shepherds giggled. After she dismounted, the donkey turned and nipped one of the sheep on its rear end, starting a brawl. The animals butted each other. A baby goat chewed on Joseph's microphone as he sang, "Joy to the world, the Savior reigns, let men their songs employ." I started wondering how to employ songs. One of the three Kings tripped and, Joseph, grinning, continued, "While fields and floods, rocks, hills and plains, repeat the sounding joy, repeat the sounding joy, repeat, repeat the sounding joy." And here was God on earth, new-born, amidst all these distractions!

That night I dreamed again that he, the Maximum Leader, and I, were both wandering through the Cuban countryside. I tried to avoid him but, he found me and demanded my documents. Inspecting them, he informed me that my visa had expired, but that he considered himself a fair and generous New Man and was willing to let me stay. I was grateful until, walking away, across the green hills and red mud, I realized that he was laughing because he'd transformed me into a Cuban, and now I was trapped.

Araceli wrote, "We are having a dreadful time with this 'special period,' but the Maximum Leader says we must resist. Imagine!"

Isabelita sent a message saying she was blind now and could no longer write.

Daniel wrote, "In Cuba this year, the winter is like spring!"

Two days after Christmas the Associated Press reported that Cuban authorities had seen a human figure clinging to the wheel carriage of a Marazul charter flight which was returning to Miami after one of the State-authorized visits of fifty Cuban-Americans to relatives on the island. Upon arrival in the U.S., the plane had been inspected by F.B.I. agents, who reported finding only traces of human blood.

The world seemed upside down. I rode my horse, and wrote down the hoarded words of Miguelito's silence and Gabriel's memory.

At night I dreamed I was inside my cousin's crumbling house with Miguelito and Aurora. Bullets came flying in through the open windows and demons were screeching.

I began to search the Bible for explanations, seeking a new message. I started at the beginning and worked my way forward. A parable in Judges 9 caught my attention. It was about the way trees went forth to choose a king to reign over them, but only the bramble would agree to take the job, threatening to explode into flame unless all the other trees would take refuge in its shade.

In Psalms I read, "I am but a pilgrim here on earth: how I need a map" and in Hebrews, "Don't forget about those in jail. Suffer with them as though you were there yourself."

I read all the way through to the end. The truth will set you free. A flaming star called Bitterness. A time when men will wish to kill themselves but will find themselves unable to carry out the act. Locusts with human faces wearing gold crowns, looking like horses and stinging like scorpions.

The human rights bulletins kept arriving. Finally I received one documenting the arrest and torture of soldiers on the tail of the alligator, near the Captive Town of Ciudad Sandino. The soldiers had been arrested by State Security after refusing to capture a man found hiding in nearby caves. The man had a homemade explosive device hidden in his pocket. He was convicted of terrorism and was executed by firing squad against the Big Wall of a medieval castle. I recognized his name as that of Gabriel's grandson, the one I'd always known simply as Taíno.

On New Year's Day, 1992, my uncle Juan traveled to the West from New York and visited us in our rural home.

"This is nice," he said to my husband, "very nice. You have electricity. You have plumbing. You have cable television and no one bothers you."

My husband, whose ancestors had lived in the U.S. for centuries, looked at me curiously and whispered, "Electricity? Plumbing? Is he really surprised?"

Suddenly I realized that, as a Cuban exile, my uncle Juan had assumed that any rural area would be like the Cuban countryside, primitive, dangerous, no witnesses.

"I will tell my mother how nice this is," Juan promised me. "She believes you live in a very small, very old cabin far back in the brush where it is very uncomfortable and all the houses need many repairs. *En el monte.*" In the mountains. Frogs. Worms. Soil the color of blood.

Suddenly I understood why they had reached the U.S. and headed straight for the biggest, most crowded and anonymous city they could find. Suddenly I knew why I had been raised in Harlem. Now I could imagine how Northerners would feel if the U.S. Army came marching across Iowa or Arizona, arresting farmers and relocating them to captive towns, executing some as examples, torturing those who were known to be the cousins of troublemakers, leaving the bodies slumped against impromptu firing walls in downtown Ames or Prescott.

Miguelito closed the door and moved to the center of his dark forested room. Clasping his guitar with its new strings, he settled into his father's big mahogany rocking chair and began to daydream.

Words came out of his vision. A wailing Moorish melody. African drums. A passionate Andalusian rhythm and the rapid staccato stamping of heels. A Taíno chant. The rattle of gourds. The clicking of turtle shells and parrot beaks.

Trees twirled across the room, brushing against Miguelito's moustached wild-west cowboy face as he sang. Horses cantered across the green hills. Cats stood under the udders of cows waiting for the movement of human fingers to release the milk. White egrets rose above the backs of the cattle, their wings becoming sails in the wind. The sky became a sea. People clung to the fragile legs of the egrets, floating away.

Miguelito rose from his father's chair, and stepped out of the room, through a crumbling wall toward the light. He was free now, singing and free. He knew he would never kill himself now, not while songs rose from his heart and mouth. Yes, perhaps suicide was contagious but, so were melodies, memories, and words.

"I would like to go to Hawaii on vacation," uncle Juan told me, "but my wife is afraid of islands. I have been told that Hawaii is something like Cuba. The same flowers. The same fruit trees. And green, very green. But my wife, she says once you are on an island, if something happens, there is no escape. Just like in Cuba."

Juan showed me a poem his teenage granddaughter wrote about her father Juanito who died young in the North, young and unexpectedly, of the worms he brought into exile from Cuban soil, worms which had crawled up inside his flesh and consumed his heart. The poem was very good, full of sorrow and joy, a wistful poem about feeling accompanied by angels, about never being alone.

Together my uncle and I looked at the photographs I had smuggled out of Cuba. He laughed when he recognized himself smiling so proudly next to Fidel Castro Ruz, *Presidente de la República, El Líder Máximo*, The Maximum Leader.

"I have told the Americans I work with about this picture," Juan said, and they say they don't believe me. I have told them about the Olympic team, and they don't believe me. They don't know what it's like in a small country. Now they will believe me."

We looked at Havana, the sea wall, El Morro Castle, Miguel holding the baby Miguelito. My childhood self, relaxing in a homemade white cotton hammock in Isabelita's patio. My arm draped across the glistening copper neck of a colt. My childhood self on horseback, chasing Gabriel's sons as they rounded up the cattle. His small grandson Taíno, smiling shyly, a parrot perched on one outstretched finger. Gabriel standing in the corral, twirling a lariat above his head. Gabriel with an exultant smile raising his fist, shaking it at the devil.

I gave all the photographs to Juan for delivery to Amparo in New York. "These memories," he said, "will make your grandmother very happy. Sad, perhaps, but also happy."

After Juan left, I went cantering across the hills of my home, debating my same old questions of good and evil, wondering about suffering, feeling like I held, inside my mouth, a golden ball which could never be swallowed.

While my husband was in the fields and our children were at school, I listened to recordings of the passionate "Deep Songs" of Andalusian gypsies. Heels stamped, trees twirled, drums pounded, gourds rattled.

The newspapers reported that 34 Cubans escaped from the island in a hijacked military helicopter.

Three Cuban exiles floated back to the island in an inflatable dinghy loaded with explosives. They were arrested and one was shot against the firing wall. As an example, said the Maximum Leader.

A British political analyst announced that she could foresee no immediate prospects of a mass rebellion in Cuba, because everyone who could possibly lead such a movement had been arrested in advance.

Hollywood celebrities gathered in New York for a pro-Castro rally. I wondered if the famous singers and actors knew how swiftly they would lose their artistic freedom should they ever actually venture into real life on the Maximum Leader's alligator-shaped island.

I dreamed I'd received an urgent letter from Miguelito, delivered by carrier pigeon. *"Se ha quemado todo. Ya no existe."* Everything has burned. It no longer exists.

I awakened feeling both glad and afraid, wondering exactly which part of everything had burned and when.

Then, the next afternoon, when the mail arrived, I really did receive a message from Miguelito which had somehow been smuggled out of Cuba and bore the postmark of a town in Louisiana. "Forgive us our silence," the message stated. "We love you very much." Crumpled up inside the folded message, I found a song, a ballad about Gabriel's grandson Taíno and Araceli's brother, during their moment of confrontation in the caverns, the moment when they recognized each other as cousins and, Taíno decided not to light his homemade bomb, and Araceli's brother decided not to arrest him.

I felt like I held a massive golden ball inside my mouth. I felt Cuban.

Re-reading the Bible, this time from back to front, I leafed farther and farther back, until finally I found, in 1 Kings 19:11-12, the passage which answered my question:

"The Lord said, 'Go out and stand on the mountain in the presence of the Lord, for the Lord is about to pass by.'

"Then a great and powerful wind tore the mountains apart and shattered the rocks before the Lord but the Lord was not in the wind. After the wind there was an earthquake, but the Lord was not in the earthquake. After the earthquake came a fire, but the Lord was not in the fire. And after the fire came a gentle whisper."

After reading the answer to my question, I stepped outside into the light and, there, waiting patiently at my door was a sunburned young woman who spoke quietly in Cuba's rapid, golden-ball Spanish.

"I am the wife of your great-uncle Gabriel's grandson," she murmured. "I come from the Captive Town seeking shelter. This is my child in my arms, a boy born at sea. I call him Angel because an angel of the Lord carried us across the sea. First we floated across the water with sharks snapping at our legs. The sun scorched our skin. The salt consumed our flesh. Then we were lifted up, and we soared as if carried by wings. And now here we are, waiting."

And just as I was about to ask, "Waiting for what?" she swallowed her golden ball and answered, in a clear and penetrating sing-song voice, a voice like a bell, a wild-bird voice which read my silent thoughts and fears and joy, "Waiting for an end to the battle which was already won before it began."